A Powerful Pucker

She grabbed for the box. Jennifer clung to it for a moment, but Sharra was tugging at it, and Jennifer was afraid it was going to break and spill Bufo onto the ground. "All right," she said grudgingly. "Take a look. But be careful."

"Oh, it's only a toad," said Sharra. "You can get another one anytime you want." Lifting the lid, she looked inside. "Just what I thought," she said triumphantly. "He looks just like you. A toad for a toad. You make a good pair."

Before Jennifer could recover from the sting of Sharra's words, Bufo leapt from the box and planted a great, warty kiss on Sharra's lips.

"Yuck!" cried Sharra. Dropping the box, she began to rub at her mouth, gagging and spitting. At the same time the sky went dark. A great bang shook the air, followed by a flash of light and a puff of smoke.

Jennifer and Ellen began to cough. They waved their hands in front of their faces to clear away the smoke.

When the smoke cleared, it was Jennifer's turn to scream. . . .

THE MAGIC SHOP BOOKS
by Bruce Coville

The Monster's Ring
Russell Crannaker, bullied all his life,
gets a chance to fight back when he is given
a monstrous magical item.

Jeremy Thatcher, Dragon Hatcher
Jeremy Thatcher's deepest desires take flight
when he is forced to raise a demanding
dragon hatchling.

Jennifer Murdley's Toad
Jennifer Murdley, a girl "in a plain brown wrapper,"
buys a talking toad who knows a thing or two about
the true nature of beauty.

The Skull of Truth
Charlie Eggleston, who can't help lying,
suddenly must tell the truth and nothing *but* when
he takes the Skull from Mr. Elives' shop.

Juliet Dove, Queen of Love
Shy Juliet Dove suddenly becomes the most
popular girl in school when she wears the ancient
amulet given to her at the magic shop.

Jennifer Murdley's
Toad

Jennifer Murdley's Toad

A MAGIC SHOP BOOK

Bruce Coville

ILLUSTRATED BY
GARY A. LIPPINCOTT

MAGIC CARPET BOOKS
HARCOURT, INC.

ORLANDO   AUSTIN   NEW YORK   SAN DIEGO   LONDON

www.HarcourtBooks.com

First Magic Carpet Books edition 2007

Magic Carpet Books is a trademark of Harcourt, Inc.,
registered in the United States of America and/or other jurisdictions.

The Library of Congress has cataloged the hardcover edition as follows:
Coville, Bruce.
Jennifer Murdley's toad/by Bruce Coville;
illustrated by Gary A. Lippincott.
p. cm.
"A Magic Shop Book."
Summary: When an ordinary-looking fifth grader purchases a talking toad, she
embarks on a series of extraordinary adventures.
[1. Magic—Fiction. 2. Toads—Fiction.]
I. Lippincott, Gary A., ill. II. Title.
PZ7.C8344Jd 2002
[Fic]—dc21 2002024107
ISBN 978-0-15-204613-2
ISBN 978-0-15-206246-0 pb

Text set in New Baskerville
Designed by Lydia D'moch

A C E G H F D B

Printed in the United States of America

*For all the beauty
victims*

Contents

ONE

The Kid in the Plain Brown Wrapper

If Jennifer Murdley hadn't been forced to wear her brother's underpants to school, the whole thing might never have happened. But when she walked into the laundry room on the morning of October 13th, she found her father pouring liquid detergent onto a load of clothes that included every pair of underwear she owned.

"Dad!" she screamed. "Wait!"

She was too late. The tub was filling, her underwear was soggy and soapy, and there was no chance of getting any of it dry before she had to leave for school.

"Don't worry," said Mr. Murdley, holding up a stack of neatly folded underpants, "you can wear a pair of these!"

"You have got to be kidding! Those belong to Skippy!"

The conversation that followed wasn't pretty. The bottom line had been that Jennifer *was* going to school, and she *was* going to wear underwear, even if it did belong to her brother.

Although she promised Skippy to keep it a secret, Jennifer confided the embarrassing truth to one person—her best friend, Ellen.

Ellen, not unnaturally, thought it was funny.

So she told Annette.

Annette told Maya.

Maya told Sharra.

And Sharra, as could have been expected, told the world.

By recess every boy in the fifth grade knew Jennifer's secret. They chased her around the playground, chanting, "Jennifer Murdley went to France, wearing her brother's underpants," while Sharra and her friends stood in a circle, giggling and pointing.

As if that weren't bad enough, when Jennifer passed Skippy in the hallway later that day, as her class was leaving art and his was entering, he hissed, "You *die,* creepazoid."

The day reached a new low when Jennifer's teacher, Mrs. Hopwell, assigned an essay on "My Favorite Pet."

Jennifer had four problems with the essay:

First, she still hadn't finished her last writing assignment, a report on Smokey Hollow's only tourist attraction, the Applegate Folk Museum. In fact, she was supposed to visit the museum that afternoon for some final research.

Second, the new topic just didn't interest her.

It wasn't that she didn't like writing. Jennifer loved to write; she just hated wasting her time on stuff that didn't come from inside her.

Third, she didn't even have a pet, which was one of the things that made the topic so uninteresting.

Fourth, and most painful, was the fact that the topic itself had prompted Sharra to whisper loudly, "I bet Jennifer has a pet horse. Why else would she be wearing Jockey shorts?" which had led Jimmy Cortez to crack, "Jennifer doesn't *own* a horse, she just *looks* like one."

Jennifer hadn't cried; she hadn't let herself. By now she was used to remarks about her looks.

I'm just the kid in the plain brown wrapper, she told herself on good days. *So ordinary, no one notices me at all.* But on bad days, like today, she was convinced that everyone *did* notice the pudgy cheeks, small eyes, and clump of a nose that made her hate her own looks so much.

She couldn't wait for school to end so she could head for the Folk Museum—though the fact that the point of this visit was research for an overdue assignment made the trip less enjoyable than usual. Still, the museum was one of her favorite places. She loved the ever-changing displays of folk art, the huge collection of apple dolls, the handmade stick brooms, and, best of all, the collection of books that covered everything from local legends to folklore from around the world.

More than that, when Jennifer was at the Folk

Museum she felt safe in a way she rarely did, as if it was a place removed from everyday worries and fears.

And this afternoon she wanted to feel safe.

When the final bell rang, Jennifer slipped away from school fast enough to avoid any more teasing, then ran the seven blocks to the museum. After a pause to catch her breath, she opened the door and stepped inside.

Once past the mirror in the foyer (Jennifer *hated* mirrors), it was easy to forget the outside world in the beautiful old house the Applegate family had donated to the people of Smokey Hollow.

The museum was still run by old Miss Applegate, the only living member of the family. Jennifer always felt kind of sorry for the woman. With her bulgy eyes and squat figure, she was truly unattractive. But she was also somewhat reassuring, since Jennifer was always able to look at her and think, *At least I don't look that bad.*

Except in her heart she suspected that she did.

"Hello, dear," said Miss Applegate, when she spotted Jennifer. She smiled. Jennifer smiled back. Miss Applegate had become a special friend over the last year.

When Miss Applegate announced that it was closing time, Jennifer was shocked to realize that she was nowhere near finished with her research. Her problem was that the material was so interesting she kept getting carried away and reading far past the relevant sections.

"Don't worry, dear," said Miss Applegate. "I'm coming in to do some extra work on Saturday morning. You can finish up then."

Since the museum was closed on Saturdays, this was a real privilege. "Thanks!" said Jennifer as she tucked her pencils and notebooks into her backpack.

Jennifer was so pleased with her trip to the museum that she almost forgot the underwear fiasco—until she reached the corner of Oak and Main, where Sharra was hanging out with a group of her friends.

"Hey, it's Underwear Woman!" cried one of them.

"Oh, shut up," said Jennifer, who had had all the teasing she could stand for one day. "At least *I'm* wearing some!"

"I bet she's not!" cried Sharra. "I bet she's lying. Let's find out."

Immediately four girls lunged at Jennifer, who turned and ran for all she was worth. From a distance she could hear Sharra urging the others to chase her. Sharra was too dignified to run herself, of course. She would wait until the others caught Jennifer and then lead whatever torture came next.

I've got to get out of here, thought Jennifer desperately as she cut a sharp right onto Beech Street. Halfway down the street she shot into a driveway. Darting behind the house, she raced through several backyards, out past another house, and between a pair of small mountain ash trees.

When she stopped to catch her breath, she

realized she was on a street she had never seen before. That made her slightly nervous, since she thought she knew all the streets in Smokey Hollow.

She listened to see if Sharra's gang was still after her.

Silence.

That was a relief.

Her heart still pounding from the chase, Jennifer walked on. It was only when she was halfway to the end of the street that she noticed the little shop.

ELIVES' MAGIC SUPPLIES
S. H. ELIVES, PROP.

read the old-fashioned letters on the window.

Jennifer felt a tickle of nervousness. She had a sense that something strange was about to happen. Something special. Maybe something she could write about. Not for Mrs. Hopwell, but for herself, just because she wanted to—which was the best kind of writing, anyway.

She looked around. The street was deserted. After a moment of hesitation, she slipped into the shop.

It was wonderful; a fascinating display of Chinese rings, top hats, oversized cards, and other magician's equipment hung from the walls, lay scattered on the shelves, and sat crammed in big display cases.

Moving aside a chain of jewel-colored silk

scarves, Jennifer ran her fingers over a dark wooden box that had a dragon carved deep into its surface. She was turning to examine the much bigger box nearby—clearly made for sawing people in half—when she noticed the wall lined with cages.

Most of the cages held doves and rabbits—for pulling out of hats, she guessed. But some of the cages had far more interesting animals: lizards, snakes, toads, and bats. Beyond the wall of cages was one more animal, a stuffed owl that sat perched on the huge, old-fashioned cash register at the back of the room.

Maybe I can get a pet for my essay, thought Jennifer, trying to imagine what her mother would say if she came home with a bat.

Wondering if there was a bell next to the cash register to call for a clerk, she began walking toward the counter. As she did, the owl twisted its head and looked straight at her. It uttered a low, eerie hoot, blinked, and returned to its original motionless position—so precisely that Jennifer still wasn't sure whether it was alive or some mechanical gadget.

"Peace, Uwila," snapped an impatient voice from the back of the shop. "I know she's there."

Moments later an old man shuffled through the beaded curtain that covered the doorway behind the counter. As he stepped through, the strings of beads blew outward, and Jennifer caught the scent of an ocean breeze—which surprised her, since the ocean was hundreds of miles away. But any thoughts about the ocean were washed away by her interest in the old man himself, who was so wrinkled he made her think of the apple dolls at the Folk Museum. Stopping directly in front of her, he peered at her intensely, paused for a moment, then said, "Well?"

Jennifer realized she had been staring. Blushing a bit, she replied, "I'd like to buy one of your animals."

"Which one?"

"I don't know yet." Glancing at the unmoving owl, she asked hopefully, "Is he real?"

The owl shook its feathers and squawked. The old man frowned. "Uwila is very real, but not for sale."

Jennifer sighed. An owl would have been nice. On the other hand, it would have been hard to care for. Probably she should go for something simple.

"What about the toads?" she asked.

The old man shook his head. "I doubt you want one of them. They're a hundred dollars. Each."

It was Jennifer's turn to squawk. "A *hundred* dollars?"

"That's what I said," the old man replied, his voice testy.

"But they're only toads."

"I am well aware that they are toads. I would not call them 'only' toads; that offends them. And the price is as I said."

"I'm not going to pay a hundred dollars for an old toad!"

"I wouldn't expect you to. Nor would I sell you one if you were willing to. They are strictly for magicians, and I don't think you qualify." He paused, then cocked his head, almost as if he were listening to something. After a moment he said, "I do have one toad—only one—that I can let you have for a somewhat lower price."

"How much?" asked Jennifer suspiciously.

"Seventy-five."

"Dollars?"

"Cents."

Jennifer scowled. "What's wrong with it?"

"There is nothing wrong with *him*. He simply does not suit my needs. He will, however, provide you with a great deal of—amusement. It may, indeed, be a perfect match."

Something about the way the old man said this struck Jennifer as odd. She had an uneasy feeling that he was making fun of her. Yet there was no trace of a smile on his face.

"What do you mean?" she asked. "Why will he be perfect for me?"

The old man shrugged. "No one comes into this shop by accident," he said, as if that explained things.

Jennifer hesitated. The old man—Mr. Elives, she assumed—was clearly a wacko. But the toad might be just right for her essay. And she could always get rid of him after she was done writing. "Okay," she said, "I'll take him."

"Don't you want to see him first?"

"Why? A toad is a toad, right?"

Now the old man did smile. "That's why I wouldn't sell you one of the others." Then he looked her straight in the eye and said, "Stay here. I'll be back in a moment."

Turning, he shuffled back through the strings of beads. Jennifer tried to move, but her legs felt as if they had been frozen to the floor. She was about to yell for help when the old man returned. He was carrying a small cage in his wrinkled hands. Inside the cage was a huge toad.

Mr. Elives put the cage on the counter. "This is Bufo."

Jennifer found she could shift her feet again. "Bufo?"

Mr. Elives scowled. "Yes, Bufo. Do you want him or not?"

Something about the old man's voice told Jennifer that if she knew what was good for her, she would want the toad. Digging her change purse out of her backpack, she extracted three quarters and handed them to the old man.

"Good," said Mr. Elives. He rang up the sale on the ancient cash register, then took a cardboard box from beneath the counter. Lifting Bufo from his cage, he deposited him in the box. He locked the box's top flaps together. Air holes had already been cut in the top and sides.

Jennifer expected him to hand her the box. Instead, he held out a carefully folded piece of paper. Hesitantly, Jennifer took hold of it. The old

man didn't let go; he just stared directly into her eyes. Jennifer wanted to turn her gaze away, but her eyes seemed to be locked in place.

"Read this paper carefully," said Mr. Elives, his voice low but intense. "Pay close attention to what it says. And take good care of this toad. If you don't, you'll have me to answer to."

Jennifer shivered. She tried to take the paper, but Mr. Elives still wouldn't let go of it. "Did you hear me?"

Wide-eyed, Jennifer nodded.

"Good." Releasing his hold on the paper, he pushed the box toward her. "Take the side door. It will get you home more quickly."

Grabbing the box, Jennifer shot out the side door. To her astonishment, she found herself back on High Street.

For a moment, she wondered if it had all been a dream. Then she realized that she was still carrying the box and the paper. So it was no dream. "What's going on here?" she asked aloud.

"You got me, kid," croaked a gravelly voice from inside the box.

TWO

A Beast
of Bufine Beauty

Jennifer blinked and stared at the box. Obviously the voice couldn't have come from there. But when she looked around, there was no other person in sight.

"Who said that?" she asked timidly.

"I did," came the voice from the box.

Jennifer closed her eyes and tried to count to ten. Before she could finish, the voice bellowed, "Hello out there! Did you hear me?"

"I heard you!" shouted Jennifer. "Where are you?"

"Right here! In the box!"

Jennifer took a deep breath, then lifted the box and peered through one of the side airholes. By the light that filtered in through the holes in the top, she could see the toad looking back at her. "Hi!" it croaked, lifting its right front leg and waving to her.

Jennifer moved the box away from her face and

squeezed her eyes shut. Then she looked back through the hole.

"Are you going to speak to me or not?" demanded the toad.

Jennifer dropped the box and ran. But she stopped at the corner. *What are you afraid of, Murdley?* she asked herself. *A talking toad is weird, after all, but he is only a toad. It's not like he's going to hurt you. Besides, you wanted a pet that was special. What could be more special than this?*

She turned around. The box lay on the sidewalk where she had dropped it. Trying to look casual, she sauntered back and bent to pick it up.

"Were you speaking to me?" she whispered.

"Yes, I was," said the toad. "And I must say, I don't think much of the way you ran off. It's a good way to kill a conversation. As for *dropping* me—well, you'd better hope word of *that* bit of foolishness doesn't get back to you-know-who!"

"I'm sorry," said Jennifer. "I was frightened."

The toad looked unconvinced.

"Really," said Jennifer. "I just got scared."

"I suppose I can overlook it this time," grumped the toad. "But don't let it happen again!"

"It won't!" said Jennifer sincerely. Looking around nervously, she tucked the box under her arm and began to walk toward her house.

"Where are we going?" asked the toad.

"Home."

"Good. This box is uncomfortable. I trust you have a nice place ready for me."

"Not exactly," said Jennifer, feeling uncomfortable herself. "After all, I didn't know you were coming."

The toad sighed heavily.

"But I'm sure we can fix something up," added Jennifer quickly.

"I certainly hope so," said the toad.

Jennifer entered the house quietly. For one thing, she wanted to get the toad settled in her room. For another, she didn't want to face Skippy any sooner than she had to.

She could hear her father out in the garage, twanging away at the piano he was restoring.

The rest of the house was silent.

She took the toad up to her room and let him out of the box. He was a handsome specimen, almost as large as the palm of her hand. His bumpy skin was not the typical dusty brown, but instead seemed to have all the colors of well-grained wood. His eyes were bright and clear, and his legs were strong. All in all, a fine figure of a toad. Jennifer said so.

"Why, thank you," responded the toad. "I'm glad you have an eye for bufine beauty."

"Pardon me?"

"My toadlike qualities."

Jennifer paused. She had never particularly thought of "toadlike" and "beauty" as words that belonged together. "What kind of a cage would you like?" she asked, in an attempt to change the subject.

"Cage?" croaked Bufo. His eyes bulged out as

if he were being squeezed. *"Cage?* What is this—a home or a prison?"

"I don't understand," said Jennifer, taken aback by his reaction. "You were in a cage at the magic shop."

Bufo hopped across the desk, pointed a finger (*Or is it a toe?* she wondered) at Jennifer, and shook it under her nose.

"That was a temporary condition," he said fiercely. "If we are to get along, you had better understand that I am not a pet. I am, for the moment, a guest. Possibly a friend. Certainly a responsibility, since you removed me from the shop. But I am most certainly not, never have been, and have no intention of ever becoming"—at this point he shivered, as if the words left a bad taste in his mouth—"a *pet!*"

"But—," began Jennifer.

"Moreover," interrupted the toad, "I did not think of my place in the shop as a cage. It was my apartment. Tiny, true, but my own. It's all a matter of how you look at things. And we are *not* going to look at my home here as a cage. Nor are we going to look at *me* as a pet! Is that clear?"

"Perfectly," said Jennifer, who was beginning to wonder if having a talking toad was going to be much fun.

"Good. Then let's try this again. A comfortable terrarium would be just fine. A big one, please— I've been feeling cramped long enough. A cozy armchair would be nice, too. Do you have one that would suit me?"

Jennifer thought of the pile of doll furniture buried in one corner of her closet. It had been there ever since the event that her family still spoke of as "Dad's Great TV Tantrum."

Actually, the tantrum hadn't been entirely Mr. Murdley's fault. He had been driven to his act of destruction when he entered the living room one Saturday morning and saw Jennifer staring at the TV set with tears rolling down her cheeks.

Wondering what his daughter found so moving, he turned to the screen, where he saw a commercial for an impossibly beautiful fashion doll.

"That was when I lost it," he explained later that afternoon. "I was just sick of that television telling Jennifer that only beautiful people matter. I love her too much for that."

Which was why he had bellowed with rage and thrown his coffee cup through the TV screen.

The next morning Mr. Murdley had appeared at Jennifer's door, holding a bumpy, brown rock that appeared to be almost perfectly round.

"What's that?" asked Jennifer.

"A geode," he said, turning the rock over so that she could see the beautiful crystals inside. They sat and talked for a long time about appearances. Later that afternoon they buried a Barbie doll in the backyard, under a tombstone that said Beauty Victim.

It was around then that Jennifer had put away most of her doll furniture.

Unfortunately, it wasn't as simple to put away her impossible desire to be beautiful.

"Did you hear me?" asked Bufo, interrupting her thoughts.

"Yes, I have a chair you can use," said Jennifer. "And I think there's a ten-gallon tank in the basement that I can turn into a terrarium. How does that sound?"

"Crummy. But if it's the best you have, I'll live with it."

"Wait here. I have to see if I can use it."

Jennifer knew her mother wouldn't be home from her law office for another hour or so. That was just as well, since her dad was more likely to give the go-ahead on the terrarium anyway; he was considerably less concerned about dirt and messes than her mother was.

Her father was still in the garage, his head buried in the back of the piano. The youngest Murdley, Brandon, was squatting next to the piano, playing with a bug. When he saw Jennifer he stood and hugged her leg.

"I'll be four soon," he said, as he had every time he saw her during the last week.

"I know, Bran," she replied, tousling his blond hair—which she would have given her right arm to have instead of her own limp, mouse-brown mess.

She waited a moment, then rapped on the side of the piano.

"Hello?" came a muffled voice from within.

"It's me, Dad. I want to know if I can have that old fish tank in the basement."

"What for?" Mr. Murdley asked, without removing his head from the instrument.

"I want to make a terrarium."

"No problem," said Mr. Murdley. "Brandon, hand me a small Phillips head screwdriver, would you?"

Brandon let go of Jennifer's leg and began pawing through the toolbox. After a moment he pulled out what his father wanted and stuck it into his outthrust hand.

"Thanks, pal," said Mr. Murdley.

"That's okay," Brandon replied, returning his attention to the bug he had been playing with when Jennifer walked up.

"Don't eat him, Brandon," said Jennifer.

"I don't do that anymore," he said firmly, picking up the bug and balancing it on his fingertip.

Hoping Brandon had really reformed, Jennifer headed for the cellar. She found the tank behind a stack of empty boxes. After lugging it upstairs, she washed it out in the bathtub, working carefully so as not to crack the glass or scratch the tub. Her shirt was soaked by the time she was done.

"Well, where have you been?" asked Bufo, when she reentered the room. "I was beginning to think you had run off and left me."

"I might consider it if you can't be a little more polite," snapped Jennifer. "I've just about drowned myself trying to clean this stupid tank for you. Honestly, sometimes you remind me of Sharra."

Bufo looked taken aback. "Who's Sharra?"

"This snobbette I go to school with. She's so stuck up she thinks she sweats perfume."

"I don't sweat at all," said Bufo smugly.

Deciding to ignore this comment, Jennifer asked, "What do you want me to do with this tank?"

Bufo's wide mouth curved in a toady smile. "Make it homey."

Ninety minutes later, Jennifer stood in front of the tank, trying to figure out where to put the last of the plants she had dug up out back. Her wet shirt was now covered with splotches of mud. A smudge of dirt ran across her right cheek to the tip of her nose. But the terrarium was looking good. A ceramic bowl formed a pool in the back corner. Next to it sat a blue chair that had once belonged to Barbie and Ken.

As Jennifer was reaching into the tank with a six-inch-wide beach umbrella, the door opened and Skippy walked in.

"Whatcha doin'?" he asked.

"Making a terrarium," replied Jennifer, annoyed that he had come in without knocking. She was also nervous; she wondered how mad Skippy was about the underwear incident. He had been hard to figure out ever since he started sixth grade.

"Where'd you get the toad?'" he asked, walking over to her desk and grabbing Bufo around the middle.

"Put him down!" cried Jennifer.

"Hey, don't get hyper," replied Skippy, lifting

Bufo into the air. The toad's legs dangled from the bottom of Skippy's fist and his chin peeked over the top; his face seemed to waver between fear and rage as Skippy raised him to look more closely.

"He's a pretty good old toad," he said, bringing Bufo's warty nose close to his own freckled one. "What do you want for him?"

"Nothing!" snapped Jennifer, grabbing for Bufo. "He's not for sale."

"Cool it," said Skippy, raising Bufo over his head, where Jennifer could not reach him. "After today, you owe me. And I say this toad is *mine*."

Still holding Bufo, he headed for the door.

"Skippy!" Jennifer cried. "Wait!"

Her brother ignored her. But as he was about to leave the room, Bufo uttered a sound that made Jennifer think of nails scraping down a blackboard.

Skippy stopped and looked at the toad in surprise. "I never heard a toad make a noise like that before," he said.

Bufo made the noise again, even louder. Skippy dropped him and stepped back. The moment Bufo hit the floor, he scrambled over to Jennifer, who scooped him up. He crouched in the shelter of her hands, glaring at Skippy.

"That toad is weird," said Skippy, looking at his hand, then rubbing it nervously on his jeans. "Are you sure he's not sick?"

"He's not sick, he's just special," said Jennifer. "And I can't give him to you because he's for a school project."

"Well, you still owe me," said Skippy. "You promised to keep your mouth shut about wearing my underpants."

"I only told one person!"

"Telling one girl is like telling the world!"

Jennifer was furious. She knew Skippy's friends gossiped at least as much as hers did, but after today's disaster she was in no position to argue the point.

"I'm sorry," she said sullenly.

"That's not good enough. Say it."

"No. Let me pay you back now."

"Give me the toad?"

"No!"

"Then say it!"

"No!"

Skippy began to reach for Bufo. "Say it, or I take the toad!"

"All right! I owe you!"

Skippy gave her a grin that she knew all too well. "Good. You can keep your old toad."

He left the room, slamming the door behind him.

"What a disgusting creature," said Bufo.

"Oh, shut up," snapped Jennifer. She was worried. To say "I owe you" was sacred in their family, a binding obligation for a favor that could be called in at any time. And Skippy was brilliant at finding the least pleasant way possible to have her cancel her debts.

"You just better be worth it," muttered Jennifer, depositing the toad in his tank.

Bufo, a shocked expression on his face, turned his back and went into a corner to sulk. Jennifer was trying to decide if she should try to talk him into a better mood, when Brandon appeared at her door. "Let's play phone," he said, holding up the red plastic phone she had given him for his last birthday.

"I'm sorry, Bran," she said. "I don't have time to play right now. I have to . . ."

Jennifer stopped. She stared at the phone her little brother was holding. It was small and made of red plastic. It had pictures of cartoon characters on the buttons.

And it was doing something it had never done before.

It was ringing.

THREE

Vocal Exercises

Brandon and Jennifer stared at the phone in astonishment.

It rang again.

"I didn't know it could do that!" cried Brandon, his voice filled with delight.

Jennifer was not as thrilled. Remembering the time Skippy had put a tape recorder under her bed and convinced her that her room was haunted, she said, "Brandon, did Skippy fix up that phone to fool me?"

"Uh-uh, no, honest!" replied Brandon, his eyes wide with innocence.

Ring!

Jennifer was not entirely convinced. Skippy had four basic ways of dealing with Brandon. They were—

a. ignoring him
b. tormenting him
c. using him shamelessly
d. playing nicely with him

Though "playing nicely" was clearly at the bottom of the list, Brandon adored Skippy, and desperately wanted to please him. So even though Brandon also loved Jennifer, it was not hard for Skippy to pull him into pranks directed against her.

Ring!

"I better answer it," said Brandon, reaching for the receiver.

"Wait!" cried Jennifer. She stared at the phone nervously. Surely the ringing had to be a prank set up by her obnoxious older brother. And yet the world had already shifted for her that afternoon. Given the fact that she had a talking toad, the idea of a toy phone that actually worked wasn't as far-fetched as it should have been.

Too bad we don't have a toy answering machine, too, she thought. Because what bothered her even more than the fact that the phone was ringing was the question, *Who's calling?* Of course, it could be Mr. Elives, with some last-minute instructions for her. Maybe he was even calling to tell her to bring the toad back. All things considered, that might be a relief.

Ring!

The more she thought about it, the more she figured it must be Mr. Elives. Who else could make a toy phone ring?

"Brandon," she said, "hand me the phone."

He shook his head. "It's my phone. I wanna answer it."

Jennifer hesitated. It might be a relief to let

26

Brandon answer it. Yet somehow it felt like a cowardly thing to do. "Bran, I really think you ought to let me answer it."

He shook his head stubbornly.

It didn't make any difference; the phone had stopped ringing.

"Phooey," said Brandon.

It took Jennifer nearly a quarter of an hour and a promise of an ice-cream cone to convince Brandon to leave the phone in her room. When Brandon decided to go see what their father was up to, Bufo scrambled over the top of the terrarium and onto the desk. "Why didn't you answer the phone?" he demanded.

"I was afraid. Besides, if you were so eager to have me answer it, why didn't you say something?"

"I try to keep the number of people I talk in front of to a minimum."

"Why?"

Bufo shrugged his warty shoulders. "People find my talking hard to deal with. It tends to frighten them."

Jennifer nodded, remembering how startled she had been when Bufo had first spoken to her.

"And since fear makes people hostile, I don't talk very much."

Jennifer snorted.

"At least among people I don't know," said Bufo, sounding defensive. "Anyway, since you didn't answer the phone, the least you can do is read the note Elives gave you. I'm dying to know what he has to say."

In the flurry of events since she had first learned that Bufo could talk, Jennifer had forgotten the note altogether. Now she fished it out of her jeans pocket. The yellowed paper crinkled in her hands as she unfolded it. Across the top in fancy letters were the words, "In Regard to Toads." At the bottom of the page was a picture of a toad. It looked smug.

Between the title and the toad was a handwritten note. The script was thin and spidery. To Jennifer's surprise, the note began with her name. That disturbed her, since she was certain she had never told it to the old man.

Feeling a little shiver in her skin, she read on.

Murdley,

As I am sure you have learned by now, the toad with which you have been entrusted has the gift of speech. Whether or not he has the gift of silence is another question. I expect things will be considerably more peaceful around my shop now that he is gone. I am old, however, and prefer my solitude. Perhaps you will enjoy his perpetual chatter.

Be that as it may, *you* must not chatter about him. Which is to say that I must forbid you to discuss him with others. At this point in the turning, the world is fairly hostile to magic. Indeed, you may well find that you are accused of truck with the devil should anyone learn that you have such a creature in your care.

And make no mistake, he is in your care, since—for reasons that have not been made clear to me—I have been requested to pass him to you.

Jennifer paused in her reading. "For reasons that have not been made clear to me." *What in heaven's name did that mean?*

"Well, what does it say?" asked Bufo impatiently.

Jennifer started to answer, but the next lines in the note had caught her eye.

Here are your instructions:

First, do not tell the toad what is in this note. He is exceedingly nosey, and a bit of mystery will do him good. Tell him I have forbidden you to repeat what is said here. He will accept that. Not happily. But he will accept it.

Second, do not speak of his existence to anyone without my permission. The toad himself may make his presence known; there is little we can do about that. You, however, would be well advised not to follow his example.

Third, be wise, wary, and watchful. I do not know why Bufo has been sent to you, but you may be certain that there is a reason. There may be danger involved.

Fourth, remember that not everything is as

it seems: the inside is not the same as the outside, endings often hold beginnings, and most mirrors are mere errors.

Good luck,
S. H. Elives

P.S. You should probably be aware of one more thing. When asked a direct question, the toad can only respond with the truth.

Jennifer folded the note and stashed it in her pocket.

"Well," said Bufo, "what did it say?"

"I can't tell you."

The toad looked indignant. "What do you mean by that?"

Jennifer shrugged. "Mr. Elives forbid me to repeat it."

Bufo blinked twice, then began to pace back and forth in front of the terrarium. "Of all the nerve," he muttered angrily. "When I think of the things I've done for him. And to repay me like this! The nerve! The nerve of the man!"

Jennifer watched the toad for a moment, then returned her attention to Brandon's phone.

"Do you suppose that was Mr. Elives calling?"

"Who knows?" replied Bufo crankily. "Now that I'm around, anything is possible."

Jennifer blinked. "Do you mean that?" she asked nervously.

"Of course," said Bufo, jumping for the edge

of the tank and scrambling back inside. "Why do you ask?"

"Just wondered," she said, without specifying that the *reason* she wondered had to do with the last line of Mr. Elives' note: "When asked a direct question, the toad can only respond with the truth."

Combining that with the statement "Now that I'm around, anything is possible" was enough to make a person very nervous indeed.

Later that night, when Jennifer was trying to go to sleep, Bufo croaked, "I'm hungry."

Jennifer didn't answer.

"I'm hungry," repeated the toad, this time more loudly.

Jennifer rolled over, trying to ignore him.

"FEED ME!" bellowed Bufo.

"Be quiet!" hissed Jennifer, sitting up in her bed. "You'll wake my parents."

"Well, I'm hungry," muttered Bufo peevishly.

Jennifer sighed. "What do you want to eat?"

"Flies!"

"Don't be disgusting. Besides, I don't have any."

"Then I'll settle for some raw hamburger."

Sighing again, Jennifer got out of bed and poked her feet into her fluffy bunny slippers. A few minutes later she was back with a bit of hamburger.

"Thanks, sweetheart," said Bufo in an odd voice as Jennifer placed the meat in the terrarium.

"What did you call me?" she asked, yanking her hand away.

"Sweetheart," said Bufo in that same odd, throaty voice. Then, seeing the look on her face, he added, "Oh, don't get nervous. I'm not going to ask you to kiss me to break a spell or anything like that. I am *not* a prince in disguise."

That was a relief. Jennifer had been half expecting the toad to ask her for a kiss all day. Without realizing it, she wiped her lips. "Then why did you call me sweetheart?"

Bufo looked crushed. "You didn't recognize that?"

"Recognize what?"

"My Humphrey Bogart imitation! I was doing Bogey and you didn't even know it!" He turned away from her, his bumpy brown shoulders slumping morosely. "Gad, this is humiliating."

"But I don't even know who Humphrey Bogart *is*," said Jennifer, bewildered.

Bufo whirled around. "You don't know Bogey? What do they teach you in these schools?"

"Not much," said Jennifer glumly.

"I should say not," snorted Bufo. "Not knowing a great actor like Humphrey Bogart . . . it's . . . it's . . . *appalling!*"

"An actor?" Jennifer loved movies. "Does he have a new film coming out?"

"He's been dead for decades."

Jennifer's face fell. "Then what good is he?"

"That's the problem with the youth of America," said Bufo, his voice totally different from before. "They have forgotten how to honor the past."

Jennifer's eyes widened. "I know that voice! It's the president!"

"It's nice to know you're not *totally* ignorant," said Bufo.

"Don't be so rude. How do you do that?"

"It's my birthright," he said in a high voice. "I'm a tongue toad."

Jennifer's eyes grew even wider. "That's *my* voice!"

She put her hand to her throat, as if to make sure her voice box was still there.

Bufo beamed at her. "You got it, kiddo," he said, doing Bogart again.

"Can you do anyone?" she asked, fascinated.

"Anyone or anything. I do a mean tiger, a superb hyena, and a pitch-perfect humpback whale. I also do traffic sounds, jackhammers, and chainsaws. Wanna hear my version of Niagara Falls?"

"Yes," said Jennifer, fascinated. "I mean, no! You'll wake up my parents."

Bufo shrugged. "Some other time," he said in his own voice. "Right now, I want to eat my hamburger."

"Be my guest."

"I am," replied the toad smugly.

But Jennifer didn't hear him. She was heading for her bed, one thought bouncing through her head: *I wonder if he can imitate Sharra Moncrieffe?*

The thought stayed with her as she drifted off to sleep. After a while she dreamed, a familiar dream in which she was the most beautiful girl in the school. She loved the dream because of the way it made her feel, and hated it as well, because sometimes it was so vivid that when she woke up and went into the bathroom she was shocked to see her real face.

In her dream she heard someone weeping. After a while she realized it wasn't in the dream after all. Someone *was* weeping. She opened her eyes. The room was dark.

The weeping continued.

It took her a moment to realize that it could only be coming from Bufo.

FOUR

The First Kiss

Jennifer slept fitfully for the rest of the night. She wanted to speak to Bufo, but it was clear that he thought that she was asleep and could not hear him. She had cried in the dark enough times herself to know that he wouldn't appreciate being questioned.

She dreamed, off and on, of toads and princesses. When the morning sun roused her and she saw Bufo sitting on her pillow staring at her, she wondered for a moment if she were still asleep.

"It's about time you woke up," he croaked.

Suddenly Jennifer knew that this was no dream. "What are you doing here?"

"I'm bored."

"Well, it's not my job to entertain you!"

"Don't you want me to feel welcome?" asked the toad, pitching his voice a little higher. He seemed to be on the verge of tears. After what she had heard last night, Jennifer might have fallen for it, if she hadn't heard that same voice in an old movie the weekend before.

"Drop the Shirley Temple imitation," she snapped. "It doesn't suit you."

Bufo looked sullen. "I'm still bored," he said, this time in his own voice.

Jennifer hesitated for a moment. "Well, you can come to school with me if you want," she said at last. "That is, if you think you can behave."

"School!" Bufo cried. "Ack! Gag! Barf!" He turned around and began to make throwing-up noises.

"Oh, calm down," said Jennifer. "If I can cope with it, you can."

"I was merely expressing an opinion," said Bufo. "I would be pleased to accompany you on your day's rounds."

Suddenly Jennifer wondered whether she should have kept her mouth shut.

"That's the first time I ever saw someone get oatmeal in his own hair," said Bufo as they headed down the front steps after breakfast.

"Neatness is not Skippy's specialty," said Jennifer.

Bufo was riding on her shoulder, so they could talk while they walked. If they saw anyone else coming, he was to go into the shoe box she had tucked under her arm.

They had walked a few blocks, chatting companionably, when he muttered, "Trouble at ten o'clock!" His voice sounded like that of a bomber pilot in an old movie.

"Huh?"

"There's someone ahead and to your left," he said, sounding exasperated.

Looking in the direction Bufo indicated, Jennifer saw Sharra Moncrieffe heading straight toward them. Scooping Bufo off her shoulder, Jennifer dropped him into the shoe box.

"Hey, Murdley!" called Sharra. "What are you wearing today—your father's boxer shorts?" Without waiting for Jennifer to answer, she asked, "What's in the box?"

"It's a toad," Jennifer replied cautiously.

"A toad! Grossamundo!"

At Sharra's cry of disgust an indignant thump sounded from the box.

Sharra's eyes went wide. "Wow. He must be a big one."

"Very," said Jennifer proudly.

"Let me see."

Jennifer eyed Sharra suspiciously.

"What do you think I'm going to do?" asked Sharra. "Steal it? Who wants an old toad, anyway?"

THUMP.

"I'm just afraid he'll jump out of the box," said Jennifer. Which was the truth, though she didn't add she was even more afraid of what Bufo might try to do to Sharra once he was out.

"Oh, you can catch him again. Let me see."

Reluctantly, Jennifer lifted the lid of the shoe

box. Bufo sat hunched in one corner, glaring murderously at Sharra.

"Oooh, he's an ugly one, isn't he?" she squealed.

Jennifer slammed the lid down as Bufo began to lunge at Sharra. She heard him thud against it and fall to the bottom of the box again.

"I like toads," she said defiantly. "If you think they're so ugly, what did you want to see him for?"

Sharra shrugged. "It's like going to the zoo."

THUMP!

Jennifer had a feeling Bufo was going to shout something rude at any moment. But before she could figure out how to break away from Sharra, she heard Ellen cry, "Hey, guys, wait up!"

Jennifer felt uncomfortable as her friend trotted up to join them. She still hadn't decided whether she was speaking to Ellen after the way she had blabbed yesterday's underwear secret.

"What's in the box?" asked Ellen.

"A huge, ugly *toad!*" exclaimed Sharra. She turned to Jennifer. "You know, you're really weird, Murdley. Why don't you get a good pet?"

"Like Ponko?" asked Jennifer sarcastically.

Ponko was Sharra's cat, and Jennifer thought the animal was just as stuck up and obnoxious as its owner.

"Perfect example!" said Sharra.

Jennifer snorted. "You got the spelling wrong. You have to put an *s* in front of the *t* in *pet* to get what Ponko really is."

Sharra glared at Jennifer. "Ponko is a purebred Persian," she said ferociously.

"A purebred Persian pest!"

"You are such a *peasant!*" cried Sharra. Flipping her long blond hair over her shoulder, she stalked away from the two girls.

From inside the box came another loud thump.

"Oh, be quiet!" hissed Jennifer.

"Boy," said Ellen, "Sharra was really mad."

Jennifer decided she was talking to Ellen after all. She had just remembered the time when she herself had accidentally told someone that Ellen was in love with Scotty Kiefer—a slip that had made a few days at least as hard for Ellen as yesterday had been for her.

"You shouldn't talk to Sharra like that," continued Ellen. "You know she'll get even some way."

"Oh, phooey," said Jennifer. "I couldn't care less about Sharra Moncrieffe and her creepy cat."

"Hear! Hear!" said a voice from the box.

Ellen's mouth fell open. "What was that?"

"Not bad, huh?" said Jennifer, forcing a laugh.

"What do you mean?"

"I mean, you didn't see my lips move. I'm learning ventriloquism."

"What?"

"*Ventriloquism.* You know—like those guys on TV who make dummies talk."

"Who are you calling a dummy?" Bufo shouted.

"Wow!" said Ellen. "That's fantastic. I didn't see your lips move at all."

"Any fool can do it!" bellowed Bufo.

40

"Oh, hush!" snapped Jennifer, whacking the top of the box. "Come on, Ellen. We'll be late for school."

"School," said the voice in the box. "Yuck!"

Later that morning Jennifer tried to concentrate as Mrs. Hopwell explained how to turn adjectives into adverbs. But with everything that had happened since yesterday, she just couldn't keep her mind on the lesson.

Additionally, she was fretting over what Ellen might say about the voice in the box. When she had told Ellen she wanted to keep her "ventriloquism" a secret until she had practiced for a while longer, Ellen had pledged her silence. But she had already failed the test of silence once this week, and Jennifer wasn't sure she could count on her.

To make things worse, Sharra, who sat two seats away, kept turning around and glaring.

What happened next would never have worked if Jennifer's desk hadn't been right under the loudspeaker. The principal had made his morning announcements a couple of hours ago, and the speaker had been silent since then. Now a sudden crackle of static was followed by his voice saying, "Attention, please."

The class grew silent. All eyes turned toward the speaker.

Jennifer wondered why people did that. *You can't see anything,* she thought. *I guess it's just something you're trained to do.*

You were also trained to expect that when you

heard the principal's voice it would come out of the speaker.

Which probably explained why she was the only one who happened to notice that Mr. Monroe's voice was actually coming from the box on her desk.

"Sharra Moncrieffe, please report to the office at once!"

A whisper rippled through the class. It was rare for Mr. Monroe to call someone in over the loud-speaker, and usually it meant big trouble. But since Sharra never got in trouble, it had to be something else.

"Sharra Moncrieffe, report to the office," repeated the voice. "And boy," it added, *are you in trouble!*

A burst of laughter sounded through the room. Sharra's face turned beet red. Mrs. Hopwell looked confused.

Sharra stumbled out of the room, looking nervous and angry. After she was gone, Jennifer tapped the box on her desk and whispered fiercely, "Knock it off, Bufo."

The only answer was the sound of contented humming.

Sharra was fuming when she returned to the classroom. She had waited outside the principal's office for two hours before the secretary finally realized there had been some mistake and that no one had called for her.

Since nobody in the class knew it had been a mistake, the room was alive with winks, nudges, and stifled giggles as Sharra slipped back through the door. The idea of Sharra Moncrieffe getting in trouble was too delicious to ignore.

Sharra cast an angry eye around the room as she moved quietly to her seat. Mrs. Hopwell, who had been correcting papers, looked up when she heard the door close.

"Is everything all right, Sharra?" she asked quietly.

"Perfectly," said Sharra. Though her voice was sweet, Jennifer could tell she was seething underneath. "It was all a mistake of some kind. I'm not in any trouble. *No trouble at all!*"

The ripple of laughter that had started around the room stopped on her last words, which were spoken so fiercely they all but dared anyone to laugh and survive.

Jennifer concentrated on drawing little boxes on her paper. She was afraid if she caught Sharra's eye she would either explode with laughter or blush with guilt, giving herself (and Bufo) away.

And that was the end of that—until shortly after lunch, when a voice from Jennifer's desk said, "Mrs. Hopwell?"

The teacher turned from the math exercise she was writing on the board. "Yes, Sharra?"

Sharra looked surprised. "I didn't say anything!"

Mrs. Hopwell glanced at Sharra strangely, then turned back to the problem of Fred's quarts and Joe's monkeys.

"Mrs. Hopwell!"

The teacher lifted her chalk from the board and turned back to the classroom.

"What is it, Sharra?" she asked, speaking very slowly and distinctly.

"Nothing," said Sharra, looking mystified.

The others were starting to giggle. Mrs. Hopwell glared at Sharra for a second, then turned back to the board again.

Sharra cast a suspicious glance around the room.

Jennifer began to squirm uncomfortably. Sharra squinted at her as if she were trying to read her mind.

When Sharra finally turned her attention back to her paper, Jennifer gave the box sitting on her desk a sharp rap with her pencil. "Bufo!" she whispered, "Knock it off!"

For a moment the room was quiet. Mrs. Hopwell glanced over her shoulder once more, looking for any sign of trouble. Nothing. She returned to the math lesson.

"MRS. HOPWELL!" roared Sharra's voice.

The class burst into laughter. Mrs. Hopwell slammed down her chalk and whirled to face the room. Her cheeks were red, her eyes angry.

"It was Jennifer Murdley!" cried Sharra, leaping to her feet. "I heard her. Jennifer's the one who did it!"

Jennifer jumped to her feet as well. "I did not!" she cried. "I didn't say a thing!"

"You did, too!" shrieked Sharra. "I know all about it. You're learning ventriloquism and . . ."

Jennifer didn't hear the rest of what Sharra had to say. She turned to look at Ellen.

Ellen was looking at her desk.

"Big mouth!" hissed Jennifer.

"So it *was* you, Jennifer," said Mrs. Hopwell. "Well, that's a highly unusual talent you're developing. But I would suggest that you find something more constructive to do with it than torment your friends and disrupt *my* classroom."

"Sharra's not my friend," said Jennifer sullenly.

Sharra fluffed her hair and looked away.

"We're all friends in this classroom," said Mrs. Hopwell. "Now, I want you to apologize to Sharra, Jennifer. And I'll see you after school."

"Sorry, Sharra," muttered Jennifer.

"Oh, that's all right," said Sharra sweetly.

Jennifer wanted to throw up.

Jennifer found Ellen waiting for her when she left the school building after receiving her lecture from Mrs. Hopwell.

"Traitor," she hissed.

"I'm sorry!" cried Ellen. "I didn't mean to get you in trouble. It's just that I was so proud of you I had to tell someone!"

Jennifer wanted to stay mad, and she didn't like the fact that Ellen's explanation made her feel better.

"So you told Annette," she said, trying to maintain her anger. "Annette told Maya. And Maya told Sharra. It's an old story. Haven't you figured it out yet?"

"I promise I'll never let out a secret again. Ever!" Jennifer could feel herself beginning to relent.

"Besides," said Ellen, "if you hadn't been trying to get Sharra in trouble, it never would have happened."

"Me!" exclaimed Jennifer. "I wasn't trying—"

A warning thump sounded from inside the box.

"Oh, forget it," said Jennifer. "It wasn't your fault, anyway." She gave the shoe box a shake and listened with satisfaction to the squawk that came from inside. "Come on, let's go home."

The two girls walked in silence until they came to the Moncrieffe house, where they found Sharra sitting on the front porch. She was holding Ponko, stroking his long white fur.

"I hate that cat," whispered Jennifer, when she noticed Ponko glaring at her.

Sharra put the cat down. "Hey, Murdley," she said. "Where'd you learn that ventriloquism thing?"

"From a friend," said Jennifer, barely slowing down.

"Wait a minute!" said Sharra, getting up from the porch. "I'm talking to you." She walked toward Jennifer and Ellen. "Gimme the box. I want to take another look at that toad."

"He's sleeping," said Jennifer nervously.

"So what? Beauty rest isn't going to do a toad any good."

THUMP.

"See?" said Sharra. "He's awake. Let me see him."

She grabbed for the box. Jennifer clung to it

for a moment, but Sharra was tugging at it, and Jennifer was afraid it was going to break and spill Bufo onto the ground. "All right," she said grudgingly. "Take a look. But be careful."

"Oh, it's only a toad," said Sharra. "You can get another one anytime you want." Lifting the lid, she looked inside. "Just what I thought," she said triumphantly. "He looks just like you. A toad for a toad. You make a good pair."

Before Jennifer could recover from the sting of Sharra's words, Bufo leapt from the box and planted a great, warty kiss on Sharra's lips.

"Yuck!" cried Sharra. Dropping the box, she began to rub at her mouth, gagging and spitting. At the same time the sky went dark. A great bang shook the air, followed by a flash of light and a puff of smoke.

Jennifer and Ellen began to cough. They waved their hands in front of their faces to clear away the smoke.

When the smoke cleared, it was Jennifer's turn to scream.

Sharra Moncrieffe was gone.

On the spot where she had been standing crouched a small, bewildered-looking toad.

FIVE

Step into My Parlor

Jennifer blinked in horror. "Bufo!" she shouted. "What have you done?"

"Jennifer, what's going on?" cried Ellen. "Where's Sharra?"

"She's right there," said Bufo, waving his front leg toward the new toad. "Cute little thing, ain't she?"

"That toad talked!" whispered Ellen, just before she fainted.

Jennifer couldn't decide whether she should try to deal with Sharra and Ellen or just run as far and as fast as she could, with the vague hope of ending up someplace where she might never be found.

Before she could give the question much thought, Ponko decided to pounce. Fortunately for the toads, Jennifer spotted the cat and caught him just as he was about to launch himself. Frustrated, Ponko turned and hissed at her.

"Cool it, fuzz brain!" snapped Jennifer, slapping him on the nose.

Bufo, suddenly aware of what was happening, squawked and jumped back into his box, which still lay where Sharra had dropped it. "Take that thing away!" he commanded, trying to pull the lid into place.

"You cool it, too!" shouted Jennifer. "I've got enough to worry about with this cat . . ."

Before she could finish the sentence, Ponko squirmed out of her grasp and dropped to the ground, landing face to face with Sharra. His hunting stance made it clear this was to be a temporary situation: soon he and Sharra would be face to stomach.

Jennifer was terrified. It was one thing to turn an enemy into a toad. It was something completely different to have her eaten by her own cat!

Fortunately, Sharra knew how to deal with her pet. "Bad Ponko!" she scolded. "Bad cat! Go away!"

The effect on Ponko of hearing Sharra's voice come out of something he was about to eat was remarkable. He hissed and fluffed his tail, then started to back away nervously. Jennifer would have sworn his eyes began to cross.

"Scat!" yelled Sharra.

Ponko yowled and took off like his tail was on fire.

For a moment no one said anything. The only sound was a soft groan from the unconscious Ellen, who was lying on the grass next to the sidewalk. Then Sharra began to scream.

"Murdley!" she screeched. "Look what you've done to me! *Look what you've done!*"

"Shhhh!" hissed Jennifer. "Someone will hear you!"

"I don't care!" wailed Sharra. "Let them hear me!"

"Spunky little thing, ain't she?" said Bufo approvingly. He was standing at the edge of his box, leaning over it like a neighbor at a back fence. "I think she looks better this way, don't you?"

"You shut up!" said Jennifer savagely. "You, too," she added, pointing to Sharra. "If you don't, someone's bound to come over to find out what's wrong. Do you want anyone to see you like this?"

"No!" cried Sharra, her voice filled with panic. "No! No! *No!* I can't let anyone see me this way!"

"Then be quiet and let me think." Plopping down on the grass, Jennifer noticed Ellen. "Wake up!" she said, giving her a nudge.

Ellen groaned, opened her eyes, took one look at Sharra, and immediately passed out again.

"Great," said Jennifer. Linking her hands around her knees to stop them from trembling, she tried to think. But her insides were churning so fast she felt like a human blender. The only thought that came to mind was, *I wonder if they can put you in jail for turning a kid into a toad?*

Sharra had begun to weep, which only made Jennifer feel worse. Much as she disliked Sharra, she didn't want her to have to spend the rest of her life as a toad.

Six months, maybe. But not the rest of her life.

Then the obvious struck her, and she wondered why she hadn't thought of it at once. "Bufo," she said. "Turn her back."

"I can't."

"What do you mean, you can't? You did it, you fix it!"

"I didn't know it was going to happen," said the toad, without the slightest touch of remorse. "She was saying rotten things, so I thought I would gross her out. I never kissed a human before. I had no idea I possessed such a powerful pucker!"

"You're a powerful fool," hissed Sharra.

"Be quiet—both of you!" yelled Jennifer.

At the sound of her shout, a man crossing at the corner paused and glanced in their direction.

Great, thought Jennifer. *Just what we need. An audience.* Scooping Sharra into her hand, she whispered, "Come on, we have to get out of here. This place is too public." But when she moved her hand toward the shoe box, Sharra jumped away, screaming, "Not in there! Not with *him!*"

"Oh, grow up," said Bufo. "Give the girl a chance to spend some time with quality and what does she do? Snub it! Well, all right for you, missy." He reached up and pulled the shoe box lid the rest of the way into place. "See if I care," he said from inside.

"You're gonna fry for this, Murdley," hissed Sharra.

"Be quiet while I think, or I'll go get Ponko."

Sharra was quiet. Jennifer thought. "Okay, look," she said at last, "we have to find someplace where we can discuss this in peace. I vote we head back to my place."

"I second the motion," shouted Bufo from inside the box.

"This is a dream," said Sharra. "I know it's a dream. It has to be a dream. Someone pinch me."

Jennifer picked her up again instead. "You can ride in the pouch in my sweatshirt," she said.

"Sure," murmured Sharra. "Why not? After all, it's only a dream. Let's go."

"First we have to wake up Ellen," said Jennifer, bending to give her friend a shake.

As it turned out, waking Ellen wasn't nearly as difficult as getting her to believe what had just happened. By the time she had managed to convince Ellen that the second toad really was Sharra Moncrieffe, Jennifer realized there was one more thing they had to try before heading for home.

"Come on," she said, when they reached the corner of Oak and Beech. "We're going this way."

"What are you doing that for?" asked Ellen, as she followed Jennifer onto Beech. "This won't take us home."

"I don't want to go home right away. I want to find the place where I bought Bufo."

"Someone *sold* you that thing?" asked Ellen in surprise.

"I'm not a thing!" bellowed Bufo. "I'm a toad. A practically perfect toad, when you come right down to it."

"If you were perfect, Sharra would still be a kid," said Jennifer, giving the box a shake.

"Don't do that!"

"Then behave," said Jennifer. Turning back to Ellen, she added, "I got him from this old man who runs a magic shop. His name is Mr. Elives."

"I've lived in Smokey Hollow all my life," muttered Sharra from inside the pouch of Jennifer's sweatshirt. "There is no magic shop in this town."

"Maybe there didn't used to be," replied Jennifer. "But there is now."

"Maybe, maybe not," said Bufo.

Jennifer stopped and lifted the lid of the shoe box. "What's that supposed to mean?" she asked.

Bufo shrugged his warty shoulders. "You don't think that shop stays in one place, do you?"

"Of course it stays in one place," said Jennifer, wishing that she really believed it.

Bufo sighed. "Look, you yourself said it's a *magic* shop . . ."

"I meant that it sold magician's supplies—you know, like it says on the window."

"Well, it does. But it *is* a magic shop. It doesn't stay in one place. It goes wherever the old man wants it to go." He paused, then added, "Or maybe where he's told to take it. I was never too clear on that part."

"Are you serious?" whispered Jennifer.

"Of course I'm serious," replied Bufo, using the president's voice for emphasis. "I don't mean you should stop looking. Just don't be surprised if you don't find it."

"But what are we going to do? We can't leave Sharra as a toad."

"What's wrong with being a toad? I've been one all my life, and it suits me just fine."

Jennifer apologized, but Bufo refused to say anything else to her. She wondered if he were really mad or actually feeling guilty about turning Sharra into a toad. Maybe he had just run out of rude comments.

Despite Bufo's warning, they spent two hours looking for Mr. Elives' shop. As Jennifer tried to retrace her path for the fourth time, Sharra began to complain.

"Listen," said Jennifer harshly. "If *your* all-girl goon squad hadn't been chasing me, I never would have come this way. And if I hadn't come this way, I wouldn't have found the magic shop. Which means I wouldn't have bought Bufo. Which means you would still be your own repulsive blond self, instead of just a ball of warts."

"Hey!" said Bufo.

Sharra began to whimper, which made Jennifer feel guilty for having lost her temper. It also made her realize that with Sharra so easily squishable, she was going to have to keep herself under control. The thought of what might happen if she got *really* angry was too horrible to contemplate.

She set her mind back to finding the magic shop. If she could only find that pair of mountain ash trees, she felt the rest would be easy. But she had been in such a blind rush to escape Sharra's gang that she couldn't remember any other markers.

"Come on, Jennifer," said Ellen. "We're not going to find anything here. We'd better go to your house—or maybe over to Sharra's."

"Not my house!" shrieked Sharra. "I can't let my parents see me like this."

"Well, we've got to tell *someone,*" said Ellen reasonably.

"No! No one! This is enough."

Jennifer was a little worried. She knew they ought to get some help—not that she really thought any of their parents would know what to do about a kid who had been turned into a toad. But it also seemed that Sharra ought to have some say in the whole situation.

It was at that moment that she found a spot that looked familiar. "I think we're on the right track," she whispered. "Come on!"

"Jennifer, I don't like this," said Ellen. "I've never seen this street before."

"That's a good sign," said Jennifer. "I told you there was something weird about this place."

"Weirder than I want to deal with," said Ellen nervously.

But though they seemed to be on the right street, there was no sign of the magic shop. In fact, the only building they saw that wasn't a private home was a small place with a sign that said Beauty Parlor hanging over the door.

"Let's ask here," said Jennifer, leading the way to the door. A small bell tinkled as she stepped into the parlor. The first thing Jennifer noticed about the place was that it was lined with mirrors. She tried to turn away from her reflection, but it seemed that no matter where she looked, she saw herself.

I can't wait to get out of here, she thought.

The shop was deserted except for a woman sitting at a desk near the front. She was applying dark red polish to her long nails and appeared to be so intent on the task that she hadn't noticed them entering. But when Jennifer cleared her throat, the woman looked up in such a slow, deliberate way that it seemed she had been aware of their presence all along.

Indeed, it was Jennifer who was surprised, for the woman was the most beautiful person she had ever seen. Her jet black hair, parted in the middle, fell about her shoulders in thick curls. Two thin black brows divided her high, pale forehead from a pair of almond-shaped eyes that seemed first green, then gold, depending on how the woman moved her head. Her smile left Jennifer sick with jealousy and wondering if this beauty parlor had any secrets that could work on her own dumpy face.

"Can I help you, girls?" asked the woman, in a voice that was like bells ringing and waves kissing the shore and children laughing.

Can you make me look like you? Jennifer wondered. Out loud she said, "Do you know if there's a magic shop on this street? I thought I saw one around here the other day."

"Are you sure it wasn't this place?" asked the woman.

Jennifer wrinkled her brow. "What do you mean?"

The woman laughed, a wonderful laugh. "Is anything more magical than beauty?"

Probably not, thought Jennifer bitterly. But aloud she said, "No, it was a little shop where you could buy magic stuff. I want to find it again."

"Tell me a little more about it," said the woman. Her voice was light, but it was forced lightness.

Jennifer shrugged, starting to feel uneasy. "It was a neat place," she said, falling back on vagueness. "I liked it, sort of."

"Did you buy anything there?" asked the woman.

This time not even the lightness of her tone could mask the hunger beneath her words. The green-gold eyes had changed again. Now they were gray, the color of cold steel.

Jennifer's skin grew cold, too. She suddenly knew that she was in big trouble, though exactly what kind she couldn't tell.

Skippy Gets Hoppy

"Jennifer, I think we should go," said Ellen, plucking at her arm.

Jennifer agreed, but she wasn't sure she could get her feet to move. They felt as if they had been embedded in cement. The woman's eyes, shifting now to an icy blue, seemed to be burrowing into her soul. Smiling, a summer sun beneath the arctic ice of her glare, the woman said, "I asked if you bought anything." Glancing significantly at the box, she raised one elegant eyebrow and added, "Anything . . . *interesting?*"

Jennifer knew she shouldn't speak of Bufo— and not only because Mr. Elives had specifically forbidden it. Something deeper, instinctual, told her not to mention him to this woman. But the woman's gaze was so compelling, the silk and steel of her voice so frightening and comforting all at once, that Jennifer could feel her control over her tongue beginning to loosen.

"I . . . I bought a toad," she murmured, her

face burning with shame at the weakness that let the words be pulled from her lips.

The woman's eyes glowed with triumph, making her at once more beautiful and more frightening. "And where is that toad now?" she asked, the tip of her tongue gliding across the top of her lip in a way that made it clear she already knew the answer.

Suddenly Ellen grabbed Jennifer by the elbow and spun her around. "Run!" she cried.

Free of the woman's gaze, it took no more than a heartbeat for Jennifer to recover her senses. Racing toward the door, she burst out of the beauty parlor and into the afternoon sunlight. From behind them she heard a chilling cry of rage and anger. But the moment the door swung shut, the cry was cut off, almost as if the door formed some barrier between the inside of the shop and the rest of the world.

"Murdley!" cried Sharra. "What's going on out there?"

"Jennifer!" shouted Bufo. "Get us out of here!"

She didn't need to be told twice. Grabbing Ellen by the hand, she ran for her life.

Five minutes later Ellen collapsed beneath a tree. "Enough!" she gasped. "I can't run anymore!"

"I think it's okay," said Jennifer, between deep rasping breaths. "I don't see her anywhere."

"Jennifer," said Bufo, using Mrs. Hopwell's voice, "what is going on?"

Jennifer was so startled at hearing her teacher's

voice that she almost answered. Then she realized what Bufo was doing. "Wait till we get back to the house," she said, pressing her hand against her side. "I'll tell you all about it then."

"Tell us now!" said Sharra from inside Jennifer's sweatshirt.

"At the house!" said Jennifer firmly, her resolve strengthened by the fact that it pleased her to defy Sharra.

But when they reached the house, explanations were delayed by the fact that the children had to deal with Mrs. Murdley. Jennifer hadn't been expecting that; even when she was late, she usually beat her mother home from work.

Today was one of those rare days when Mrs. Murdley had arrived home first. Even worse, she was cooking, which meant that she had probably had a bad day. Mrs. Murdley hated to cook and only did it when she wanted to let off steam by slicing up some vegetables.

"Where have you girls been?" she asked now, as Jennifer and Ellen came through the back door into the kitchen. Then she whacked the top off a carrot.

"Just out," said Jennifer.

Mrs. Murdley frowned. "Jennifer, you know I want you to check in with us before you take off after school. Your father had no idea where you were. Not that he has enough sense to get worried about you."

Since Mrs. Murdley never complained about Mr. Murdley in front of her children unless she was feeling exceptionally cranky, Jennifer knew that now was not the time to tell her that Sharra Moncrieffe was a toad and that she, Jennifer, was probably responsible. As a lawyer, Mrs. Murdley would immediately start thinking about the possible lawsuits involved.

On the other hand, thought Jennifer, *if I get arrested for this, at least Mom will know what to do.*

The thought comforted her. Not a lot, but at this point, she would take what she could get.

Gathering her courage, she asked, "Can Ellen spend the night?"

Despite her mother's mood, Jennifer knew the odds were good that she would agree to this request. Sensitive to neighborhood gossip that she was too busy with her career to be a good mother, Mrs. Murdley was always glad to have an outside witness to the times that she actually did cook.

"If it's okay with her parents," said Mrs. Murdley, decapitating another carrot.

"Thanks!" said Jennifer.

She meant it; she really didn't want to be left alone with Sharra and Bufo. Reaching up, she gave her mother a hug—which always made her feel tiny, since her mother was so tall. It also made her feel uglier than usual, since Mrs. Murdley was very beautiful.

Jennifer thought it was very unfair that such a beautiful mother could have such an ugly kid. Of course, it wasn't her mother's fault. But it sure didn't make things any easier.

"Sorry about being late," she whispered, when Mrs. Murdley bent down to kiss the top of her head.

"It's all right," said her mother softly. "But don't let it happen again. What have you got in the box?"

Jennifer shrugged. "Just an old toad," she said casually.

THUMP!

"Sounds like a big one," said Mrs. Murdley. "What are you going to do with him?"

"I wish I knew!" said Jennifer.

"All right," said Jennifer, once they were safe in her room, "let's *think*." She took Sharra out of her pouch and set her on the bed.

"Let's not," said Bufo, climbing out of his box and hopping over to his tank. "I've still got a headache from the bouncing you gave me on the way home. Have you got an aspirin I can lick?"

Jennifer hesitated. She wasn't supposed to get aspirin for herself. On the other hand, Bufo was basically an adult.

"Just a minute," she said.

"Forget it," said Bufo. "I was only kidding. They stick to my tongue. Give me a few minutes to recover. Then I want you to tell me about that woman you were talking to, what she looked like, how she acted—all the things I missed by being in that box."

He jumped for the edge of the tank, then climbed over the side and went to sit under his umbrella.

"I think we should take Sharra back to her parents' house now," said Ellen, glancing at Bufo nervously.

Jennifer's stomach twisted. Even though it wasn't really her fault Sharra was a toad, she had a feeling she was going to get blamed for it. But she also had a feeling that Ellen was right.

Sharra didn't share that feeling.

"No!" she cried. "No! No! No!"

"All right," said Jennifer, patting Sharra on the head with her forefinger. "Calm down. No one's going to force you."

"Don't do that!" snapped Sharra.

"Well excu-u-u-use me," said Jennifer, drawing her hand back.

They sat in gloom for a moment, the only break in the silence the annoying buzz of a fly.

Suddenly Sharra's tongue shot out—ZAP!—and nailed the fly.

"Good work," said Bufo.

"Aahh!" cried Sharra, jumping around on the bed as though someone had just lit a match underneath her. "Aahhh! Aahhh! Aaaahhhhh! I ate a fly! I ate a fly! I didn't want to! I didn't mean to do it! Aaahhh!"

"Oh, quit beefing," said Bufo. "They're good for you."

"Aaahhh!" said Sharra.

"Don't worry," said Ellen in a soothing voice. "It was a very natural thing to do."

"Aahhh!" cried Sharra. "Call the doctor! I ate a fly!"

"Do you *really* want us to call a doctor?" asked Jennifer.

"Yes! NO! Just do something!" Suddenly Sharra stopped moving. "If you ever tell anyone about this, I'll kill you," she said, her voice trembling with passion.

Jennifer had just been thinking how much fun it would be to tell the rest of the fifth grade about Sharra Moncrieffe eating flies.

"Promise you won't tell," demanded Sharra.

Jennifer sighed. "My lips are sealed," she said, raising one hand in a sign of pledge.

"Mine, too," said Ellen.

"Sheesh," said Bufo. "You'd think there was something wrong with eating a fly."

"Shut up!" snarled Sharra. Then she hopped across the bed, crawling halfway under the pillow, and squatted there glaring at the rest of them.

"We do have to let your parents know where you are," said Ellen, after an uncomfortable silence.

"I don't want them to know."

"If we don't say something, they're going to call the police," said Jennifer reasonably. Inside she was wondering who the Moncrieffes would call once they found out their daughter was a toad.

"So what?" said Sharra, who was clearly in no mood to be cooperative.

"Well, sooner or later the police will come over here and start asking questions."

"So? You're not going to tell them what happened."

"Of course not," said Jennifer. "But Ellen probably will. She can't keep a secret to save her life."

"Hey!" cried Ellen. "I can too keep a secret."

"Name one," snapped Jennifer.

Ellen glowered at Jennifer.

"All right," said Sharra. "You've made your point. Go ahead, call my parents."

"You'll have to talk to them," said Jennifer.

Though Sharra resisted, Jennifer finally convinced her. Which is how the three of them, Jennifer, Sharra, and Ellen, wound up out in the hall, Jennifer dialing the number, Sharra squatting next to the receiver, and Ellen keeping watch for Skippy or Jennifer's parents.

Jennifer had to admit that Sharra handled the moment well, chatting with her mother as if nothing at all was wrong. But as soon as the call was over, she lapsed into a stunned silence. Jennifer immediately began to feel guilty again. She recalled how Sharra had wept all the way home, muttering about dreams. When they returned to Jennifer's room, Sharra sat in silent gloom on Jennifer's pillow, her bulging eyes glazed over.

"At least this happened on a Friday," said Ellen, trying to sound cheerful.

Jennifer knew what she meant. They never would have gotten Sharra's parents to let her stay over on a school night.

"All right," said Bufo, "you've done your duty to little Miss Perfect's parents. Now I want to know

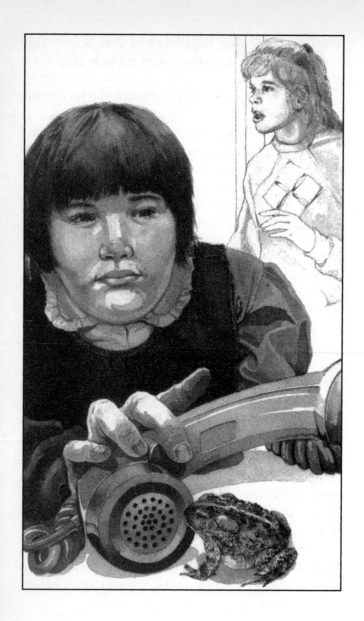

the details of what happened in that beauty parlor." He sounded nervous, which made Jennifer a little nervous, too.

"Well, you heard it all from inside the box, didn't you?" she asked.

"Of course I heard it," said Bufo. "I just couldn't *see* anything. That's why I want more details."

But before Jennifer could answer, her father's deep voice came booming up the stairs. "Jennifer, Ellen, come to supper!"

"We'll have to tell you later," said Jennifer.

"Now!" demanded Bufo.

"Don't leave me here with him!" cried Sharra.

"Later," said Jennifer again, scooping up Sharra and returning her to the sweatshirt pouch.

Between Jennifer's nervousness and her mother's bad mood, supper was a tense affair, enlivened only by the moment when Skippy stuffed a pair of string beans into his nostrils and cried, "Look! Super boogies!"

"I want boogies, too!" cried Brandon, who until that point had been refusing to even look at his beans.

Mr. and Mrs. Murdley were not amused. After supper Mr. Murdley announced that Mrs. Murdley needed a break, and he was taking her out to a film.

"Which means that the four of you are going to be very, *very* good for the next few hours, doesn't it?" he asked in a voice that could only be answered with words like, "Yes," and "Certainly," and "Of course we are."

He also told Jennifer and Ellen they could babysit for Brandon, which meant that they would be getting a little money when he got back. Usually the job would have gone to Skippy, but he had been banned from babysitting for two months after the haircut he gave Brandon the last time he took care of him.

Sharra was extremely quiet when Jennifer extracted her from the sweatshirt pouch and deposited her on the bed.

"I think she's gone into shock," said Ellen nervously.

"Story time!" said Bufo, climbing over the edge of his tank. "It's time for you to tell me the details of what happened this afternoon. Jennifer, *this is important!*"

Jennifer looked at him in surprise. But before she could answer, Skippy burst into the room. "Jennifer, have you seen my math book? I could have sworn—"

He broke off when he spotted Sharra squatting on Jennifer's pillow. "Hey, you got another one! Or is this one yours, Ellen? What is this? Are toads a new fad or something?"

Crossing to the bed, he scooped Sharra into his hand.

"Put her down, Skippy!" cried Jennifer.

"Cool it, Jen. Sheesh, I never saw anybody get

so cranky about toads. What's the big deal? A toad is a toad."

"Not always," said Jennifer. "Anyway, be careful of her."

"Why?"

"Ah—we think she's pregnant!" said Ellen desperately.

Skippy held Sharra away from him and looked at her appraisingly. "Could be," he said. "She's kinda chunky."

Sharra let out an indignant squawk. Skippy jumped and almost dropped her. "These things make the weirdest noises," he said. "What kind of toads are they, anyway?"

"She's a rare breed," said Jennifer. "Very expensive. That's why I told you to be careful."

"Sister, dear, you are getting weirder by the day," said Skippy, lifting Sharra toward his face to examine her more carefully. He poked a finger at her nose. "Man," he said approvingly, "she sure is ugly."

With a cry of indignation, Sharra lunged at Skippy.

"Hey, what—?" he cried.

Those were the last words out of his mouth before Sharra's toady lips connected with his.

"You Owe Me!"

When the smoke cleared, there were still two toads in the room.

Sharra was not one of them. Skippy, however, was. No longer tall and red-haired, he was now small, brown, and covered with warts. Jennifer was not altogether sure that this wasn't an improvement. Unfortunately, she was fairly confident her parents would not see the matter in that light. Disgusting as Skippy might be, she was certain they would rather he were a boy than a toad.

Skippy would almost certainly share that opinion, once he had figured out what had happened. At the moment, he was totally oblivious to his new shape. "Whooo-ee, what was that all about?" he cried. Coughing, he waved a warty little hand in front of his face.

That was when he realized what had happened to him.

"My hand!" he screamed. "What happened to my hand?"

This was followed by a brief pause while Skippy examined the rest of his body. This examination was followed by a series of screams, interspersed with such phrases as, "Gonna die, Jennifer," and "What are you three, witches?" and "Get me outta this!"

The only one who was actually happy about this development was Sharra.

"It couldn't have happened to a better brat," she said. Then she shook her hands and said, "Oooh, I'm all pins and needles, like when your leg goes to sleep. Except it's all over me! Ooooh!"

"I'll teach you!" cried Skippy, jumping at Sharra. It was a solid, toadlike leap, but Skippy wasn't used to his new shape, and Sharra easily dodged it. He went sailing past her calf and landed on the floor behind her.

"Jennifer!" he cried pitifully. "What's going on here?"

"And is it catching?" muttered Ellen nervously.

"Ah—it seems to be a temporary condition," said Jennifer.

"You mean I'm going to turn back?" asked Skippy, his voice flooded with relief.

"I think so. Sharra did."

"How did she do it?"

"She passed it on to you," said Jennifer, who didn't like where this conversation was going.

"Passed it on?" asked Skippy.

"You're it," said Sharra, who was still patting her arms to check that she was really herself again.

73

"It's like playing tag. I got it from that crazy talking toad of Jennifer's."

"What talking toad?" asked Skippy.

"I believe she's referring to me," said Bufo, who was now crouched on the edge of Jennifer's desk.

"Did you used to be a person, too?" asked Skippy.

"Good heavens, no!" cried Bufo. "Perish the thought. A person, indeed. Yetch. I would think you would be glad of the transformation, Master Skippy. I mean, think how much less destructive toads are than humans. We don't pollute. We don't have wars. We don't cause forest fires. About all we do is eat nasty bugs."

"Don't remind me," cried Sharra, which caused Jennifer to snort in spite of herself.

"I'm a t-o-o-o-ad!" moaned Skippy, his voice still filled with disbelief. Suddenly he scrambled under the bed.

"It's the shock stage," said Sharra, when Jennifer began to move toward the pillows. "He needs some time to himself."

Jennifer figured that if anyone should know what Skippy was feeling, it was Sharra, so she decided to leave him alone. Besides, she was in no hurry to get him thinking about everything that had just been said.

"While your brother is contemplating his lack of a navel," said Bufo, "I think it's about time you gave me some information. I've been trying to get you to tell me what happened to make you start running this afternoon."

Jennifer hesitated. Now that the incident was over, she wondered if maybe it had simply been her imagination getting out of hand.

Ellen had no such reservations. "I think that woman was a witch," she said.

Bufo's eyes bulged out even more than normal. "Tell me more," he insisted. "Everything you can remember." Then he listened with uncharacteristic silence as Jennifer and Ellen described the events in the beauty parlor.

No one spoke for a moment after they were finished. Outside a cold wind blew at the window. Colored leaves swirled along the sidewalk, flashing bright in the puddles of light from the streetlamps, then looking almost like bats when they plunged back into the darkness.

"You were probably right," said Bufo at last.

"That she was a witch?"

"Yes."

"Bufo, is there something that *you* ought to tell *us?*" asked Jennifer, who was starting to feel more frightened than ever.

Bufo glanced around nervously.

"Bufo!"

"She may be after me," said Bufo, his throat expanding and contracting rapidly.

"Why?"

"You can't live as long as I have without making a few enemies," said Bufo.

"*You* probably can't go three days without making enemies," replied Sharra.

Jennifer was torn between telling Sharra to shut up and agreeing with her.

An hour or so later Jennifer returned from putting Brandon to bed to find Skippy sitting in the middle of her floor, his warty face creased with a big smile.

"I've got it!" he cried triumphantly.

"Got what?" asked Jennifer nervously.

"The solution to my problem. I just remembered that you owe me a favor, sister dear. And not just a little favor. A *big* favor, from a genuine, unbreakable pledge. And as I was squatting there in the dust kitties under your bed, I suddenly realized just what I wanted."

"Really?" asked Jennifer. She felt her knees begin to wobble.

Skippy nodded. "It's nothing much. Just a kiss from my favorite sister."

Jennifer swallowed, but said nothing.

"You owe me," said Skippy ominously. "You said it, and you can't break it."

Jennifer closed her eyes. She felt a lump forming in her throat. A toad. She was going to have to become a toad. But what choice did she have? Skippy had the goods on her. She could refuse, but that would make her a double-down-dirty rotten-go-backer.

Was it worth becoming a toad just to keep her promise?

What was a promise worth?

What was she worth?

"I'm waiting, sister dear," said Skippy.

What was *Skippy* worth, when you came right down to it? Not much, she decided. But that wasn't the issue. What was her word worth? Of course, in a sense it was her fault that he was in his current predicament. She was the one who had brought Bufo into the house.

But to become a toad? When the one thing she really wanted to be was beautiful?

"You don't have to do it, Jennifer," said Bufo.

"Yes, she does!" snapped Skippy.

"No, she doesn't!" yelled Ellen.

"Yes, I do," whispered Jennifer. Bending over the bed, she pursed her lips and leaned toward Skippy.

Leaping up, her toad of a brother planted a kiss on her lips.

Thunder shook the room. The change began so quickly that Jennifer barely knew what was happening. A moment of intense heat, a *squashing* sensation, and the next thing she knew she was looking up at the corner of her bed—which towered over her like some oddly soft, six-story-high building.

"Whew," said Skippy, stretching his arms and examining his fingers, "what a relief that is!"

"Oh, shut up," said Ellen loyally. "In your heart you'll always be a toad."

"Hey!" Bufo cried. "I resent that."

"Shut up, yourself," snapped Skippy. "I'm not the one who brought that maniac toad into the house. He's Jennifer's problem. Wow, I feel like I've got pins and needles everywhere!"

"Don't worry," said Sharra. "It'll go away in a little while."

Ellen bent and scooped Jennifer into her hands. "Are you all right?" she asked gently, once she had raised her friend to face level.

"All right?" asked Jennifer weakly. "I'm a toad!" She tried not to let the sorrow that filled her sound in her voice. She was a toad—the very symbol of ugliness! Putting her tiny, webbed fingers against her face, she felt the warts that dotted the surface like a scattering of fleshy pebbles.

A toad!

"Hey, it doesn't have to be permanent," said Skippy. "All you have to do is find someone to kiss."

"Shouldn't be hard," said Bufo cheerfully. "She's an exceptionally good-looking toad."

Jennifer let out a wail.

"What did I say?" cried Bufo. "What did I say?"

The argument was interrupted by a sound from Jennifer's bedside table.

Brandon's toy phone was ringing again.

For a moment no one said a word

Ring!

"What's going on here?" said Skippy, his eyes wide with terror.

"Who knows what things lurk at the edge of reality?" asked Bufo, using a deep, hollow-sounding voice. "Yet this may be the ring of truth. Do you dare answer?"

Then he laughed a low, echoing laugh.

Ring!

"Not me," said Skippy, backing away from the phone.

"Bwa-ha-ha-ha-ha!" chortled Bufo in that same low voice.

"For heaven's sake, stop it, Bufo," said Jennifer. "We've got enough problems as it is. Now, is someone going to answer that or not?"

No one moved.

Ring!

"Oh, take the phone off the hook and *I'll* answer it," said Jennifer. "I'm sure it's Mr. Elives. Maybe he can help."

Looking at the phone as if it might bite her, Ellen lifted the receiver. She placed it on the bedside stand, then set Jennifer beside it.

"Hello?" Jennifer said. "Mr. Elives?" Then she hopped up to the other end of the phone to listen.

To her shock, the voice that came through the speaker did not belong to Mr. Elives. It belonged to the woman they had met in the beauty parlor. In tones that made Jennifer think of steel wrapped in silk, the woman spoke four words: *"I want the toad."*

The jolt of fear that shook Jennifer was so strong she reacted without thinking. Putting her front legs against the phone, she pushed with her powerful hind legs. The phone skittered across the polished wood and clattered to the floor.

Everyone stared at the toy phone; no one moved.

I want the toad! repeated the voice at the other end.

Then there was a click, a buzzing, and silence.

EIGHT

The Immortal Vermin

The glowing green numerals of Jennifer's clock radio said 3:14. Except for a bit of stray silver from the nearly vanished moon, the time offered the only light in the room.

Jennifer and Bufo sat side by side on the top of Jennifer's dresser.

Sharra and Ellen were in Jennifer's bed. Somewhat to Jennifer's satisfaction, Sharra was snoring. Loudly.

Brandon lay on the floor next to them. He had wandered in about midnight, as he often did, clutching his blanket and his favorite pillow. Plunking himself down on the floor beside her bed, he had inserted one thumb in his mouth and immediately fallen into a deep and peaceful sleep.

Skippy was in his own room—maybe sleeping, maybe not. Jennifer hoped not. If there was any justice, his conscience would be keeping him awake.

Her parents were most likely asleep as well. They

had come in shortly after Brandon, counted heads, assumed the two kids in Jennifer's bed were Jennifer and Ellen, and gone to their own room.

"Bufo," whispered Jennifer, "are you asleep?"

"Merely resting my eyeballs," he replied, using the voice of W. C. Fields.

"Bufo, I'm so frightened."

Bufo opened his eyes. "I don't blame you, kid," he said. "I probably would be, too. But look at it this way: It's not a bad life, being a toad. You live off the land, go where you want. Work for a wizard now and then if you feel like it. As long as you watch out for snakes and other things that want to eat you, it has some real benefits."

"Were you always a toad?"

"From the moment I happened."

"Happened?" asked Jennifer. "Don't you mean hatched? Or meta . . . meta . . . you know, changed from a polliwog into a grown-up."

"Never was hatched," said Bufo. "Never metamorphosed from a tadpole. I'm one of the Immortal Vermin, and I just—happened."

"What do you mean?"

"It's a long story."

"You planning on going anywhere soon?" Jennifer asked, her voice stubborn.

Bufo sighed. "I suppose you have a right to hear it."

"Under the circumstances, I think that's true."

"All right. But if you want to hear it, settle down and listen. No interruptions."

Jennifer thought about pointing out that, of the two of them, Bufo was far more given to interrupting than she was. She decided she was more interested in getting the story than in having a manners contest, so she simply nodded her head and said, "No interruptions."

"All right," said Bufo, "Then here we go. Once upon a time—"

"Wait a minute, I want the real story," said Jennifer, "not some fairy tale."

"Most real stories start that way," said Bufo sharply. "And I guarantee you that this story is more real than your promise not to interrupt has turned out to be."

"Sorry," said Jennifer, angry at herself for letting Bufo lure her into an interruption so quickly. She had a sense that he was testing her.

"As I was saying before I was so rudely interrupted, once upon a time there was a woman who lived in a forest. She had two daughters."

As Bufo spoke, Jennifer could hear him altering his voice, not in an imitation of anyone specific—at least, not anyone she could identify—but so that it had a storyteller's qualities. She could feel the words and the way he spoke them drawing her in. She decided to relax and enjoy the story and wait until later to decide if it was true.

"Now," continued Bufo, "one of these daughters was as good and as kind as anyone could wish, though she was surpassingly ugly. The other girl was vain, cruel, and foul-tempered, but she had a face like a nightingale's song. Guess which one the mother loved the most?"

Jennifer didn't speak.

"I said, guess which one the mother loved the most."

"I heard you!" said Jennifer. "I just didn't dare say anything because you told me not to interrupt."

"Don't be silly. Answering a question isn't the same as interrupting."

"Well, I thought you might be trying to trick me."

"What kind of a toad do you think I am?"

"That's what I'm trying to find out."

"Well, that's what I'm trying to tell you."

"Then tell me!"

"Then which one do you think the mother loved the most?"

"She loved the ugly one," said Jennifer hopefully.

"Don't be silly. She loved the pretty one."

"But you said the pretty one was mean and nasty."

"But she was pretty, which seems to count for a lot with human beings. Besides, the mother was mean and nasty, too. They were a real pair."

"I don't think I like this story," said Jennifer.

"I'm not telling it to make you happy, I'm telling it because you wanted to know where I came from. Now stop interrupting."

Jennifer fell silent.

"So, once when they were trying to make life miserable for the ugly sister, the mother and the beautiful daughter sent the poor girl out in the snow to gather strawberries, or something stupid like that. So off she goes, in her bare feet, her toes starting to freeze the minute she goes out the door, and before you know it she meets this weird old woman, who asks her for some food. So the kid gives her the only crust of bread she has, and the old woman tells her where to find some strawberries in the snow and that she will have a great blessing when she gets home. Well, the poor ugly girl finds the strawberries, heads for home, and when the mother and the sister ask where she got them, she opens her mouth to speak. And with every word a diamond or a ruby or a chunk of gold, or something like that, comes tumbling out of her mouth. Stop me if you've heard this before."

Though she had once heard a story *something* like it, Jennifer remained silent.

"Well, they think this is a good deal, so they bundle up the good-looking sister and send *her* out in the snow, too. Only this one gets plenty of food. And shoes. Naturally, she meets the old woman, too—and don't ask *me* why the old woman was standing around in the winter begging for bread, especially when she already had the bread that belonged to the first girl. Anyway, when young-and-lovely meets the old woman, she asks her where to find the strawberries, and the old woman says she will tell her, but won't she please spare some food.

So the girl says, first you tell me, then I'll feed you. But when the old woman tells her where to go, then holds out her hand for the bread, the girl just laughs at her, which goes to show you what kind of a creep she was to begin with.

"She finds the strawberries, picks until she gets bored, which was probably about three minutes, then heads for home. But when she gets there the strawberries are all rotten. And when she opens her mouth to tell her mother the whole story, with every word out pops a snake, a lizard, a rat, or some other animal that humans seem to find particularly despicable."

"And that's where you came from?" cried Jennifer.

"Don't interrupt! Anyway, as you can imagine, the young wretch finds this situation most unpleasant. Being too dumb to realize that the flood of vermin is her cue to shut up, she starts screaming for help. Of course, with every cry of 'Help!' out pops another critter—including, eventually, me. I was the first toad, and one of the very few to arrive that day." Bufo grinned. "I've always felt that our relatively small numbers in that crowd indicated that we toads are more rare and precious than those other beasties."

Jennifer tried to snort, but it came out as a croak.

"I'll ignore that," said Bufo. "Now, this arriving was a strange sensation, I want to tell you. I mean, one minute I *wasn't*, next minute I *was*—by which I mean I existed. I materialized in what felt like a dark, wet cave. Actually, it was the girl's mouth. When she opened it to scream, I was nearly blinded by the light that flooded over her lips. Suddenly I found myself hurtling toward some white rocks—her teeth—then shooting out into the air. I landed on the floor in the middle of a writhing mass of critters, all of which had come out of her mouth over the last few minutes.

"After a moment, I looked around. In the corner was this ugly girl, sitting on a table and looking oddly amused. Beside me, standing on a chair, was a nice-looking middle-aged woman, screaming at her daughter to shut up. And behind me was this gorgeous girl, dumb as a brick, eyes wide, screaming for help, with snakes, lizards, rats, and an occasional toad popping out of her mouth because she was too bone-stupid to close it.

"And the most embarrassing thing is, *she's* my mother, at least in some sense of the word.

"That, by the way, explains why I can talk, and why I am so good with my voice. I am a tongue-toad, born of this babe's flapping, temporarily unstoppable tongue.

"Actually, all of us milling around there on the floor were tongue-creatures. We were also bright enough to realize that things were about to get quite nasty, since the mother finally jumped off the chair and grabbed a broom and started whacking at us. After a moment she decided she would do better to take a whack at her daughter first, so she swung the broom around and cracked her daughter

upside the head, which knocked her out, which shut her up, which stopped the flood of tongue-beasts.

"Then the mother started trying to drive us out of the house. We were perfectly willing to go, but things were a little crowded at the doorway, what with several hundred of us trying to get out there all at the same time. So she slammed some of us with the broom pretty hard. Which was when we began to realize that it was really tough to kill us. Not impossible; she managed to knock off a few of us by total squishification. But for the most part you could give us a whack that ought to knock us into next Wednesday, and it would just slow us down a bit. This was the first hint we had of the strange fact that we were—get this—immortal. Or at least the closest thing thereto. If I get careless in the woods and let some sneak of a snake eat me, it's good-bye Bufo, forget the next act. If I get run over by a car, it's roadtoad flat out and no more toadly wit and wisdom. But barring anything like that, I am a toad who will live forever. At least, that seems likely, since I have already lived for over five hundred years."

Jennifer caught a kind of break in Bufo's voice, as if he were hovering on the edge of tears.

"Alas," he said softly, "four hundred and ninety-five of those years have been sharp-edged with sorrow, a life lived with a knife in the heart."

"What do you mean?" whispered Jennifer.

"I fell in love," replied Bufo, "with one of the Immortal Vermin, a wondrous lady named Esmerelda. She was a toad of great virtue, wise, funny, and loving. Life seemed perfect: we were young, we were in love, and we expected to live forever. But that short taste of heaven ended the day she disappeared.

"Frantic, I searched everywhere for her. The other Immortal Vermin helped. For a long time there was no word of her. Then one of the Vermin picked up a rumor: a witch was after us—specifically after the immortal toads, because she believed that hidden in our foreheads is a gem that will grant perfect happiness to whoever possesses it."

"Is that true?" asked Jennifer.

"If it is, it certainly hasn't done me any good," said Bufo gruffly. "It's possible the gem simply doesn't work for the toad who was born with it. One theory is that it has to be extracted from the forehead and given to someone."

"But is it really there?" persisted Jennifer, staring at Bufo in fascination.

"Why? Do you want it?" he asked, sounding like Darth Vader.

"No! I'm just interested is all."

"Follow me," said Bufo. He hopped across the top of the dresser, moving slowly because the space was fairly cluttered, stopping when he reached the small nightlight that was plugged into the wall. When Jennifer had joined him he turned to face her, then scrunched down, raised his front feet to his forehead, and began to pull at the skin. After a moment the skin parted. Beneath the opening, embedded in the flesh of Bufo's forehead, was a small green gem. It sparkled, even in the dim rays of the nightlight.

"Behold," said Bufo. "The Jewel of Perfect Happiness."

NINE

Osculatory Experiment

"May I touch it?" asked Jennifer.

"I'd rather you didn't," said Bufo. He lowered his toes, which let the skin close back over the opening. "Besides, I don't think merely touching it will do you any good. Certainly hasn't done much for me," he said, his voice still heavy with sorrow.

Jennifer drew back. "What happened next?"

"I continued to search for Esmerelda. The Brotherhood of the Vermin grew slowly smaller. Despite the fact that we didn't die by normal means, every now and then one of us would meet with an accident. Others simply chose to leave the forest to explore the world at large. Of course, once in a while we would discover someone new."

"Someone new?" asked Jennifer.

"A new immortal. It didn't happen very often. Once that girl knew toads and snakes would pour out of her mouth every time she spoke, she didn't say much. But I guess she still felt compelled to speak on occasion, because every now and then a handful of new immortals would enter the forest.

"After a while I decided to leave the woods. With Esmerelda gone I had no real reason to stay, and part of me had always wondered if she had grown angry for some reason and run away.

"And thus have I wandered the world for centuries, seeking my lost love. But alas, alas, not a sign of her have I seen."

Bufo sang these last words in a voice that reminded Jennifer of the wandering minstrel who performed at the Renaissance Faire the Murdleys visited every summer.

"Is that why you were crying last night?" she asked after a moment.

"You weren't supposed to hear that."

Jennifer didn't say anything.

Bufo sighed. "It's true. I was weeping for Esmerelda."

"Then you've been true to her all this time?" asked Jennifer. She was slightly amazed at the idea, since at least three families on their street had had divorces in the last year or so.

"Yes, I have," said Bufo sharply. "Not that I've had that many opportunities for hanky-panky. After all, I'm not interested in your average, garden-variety toad; I need a woman I can talk to. And there ain't that many witty, literate, immortal lady toads to be found."

Jennifer made a mental note not to say anything too witty or literate while she was still a toad.

"What were you doing in the magic shop?" she asked after a brief silence.

"A temporary haven. I had been working for wizards off and on over the years. About ten years ago I was having some trouble with my current boss and the old man took me in. I helped around the place a bit, kept track of records for him, did a few of the kinds of chores that a brilliant immortal toad is best at. Funny old coot, that Elives. I think I was at least as surprised as you were when he sold me to you."

"Why *did* he do that?" asked Jennifer.

Bufo lifted his warty brown shoulders in a shrug. "Who knows? But I've never known him to do something without a reason."

Jennifer hoped that Mr. Elives' reason didn't have anything to do with her becoming a toad and filling the hole in Bufo's life. Before she could find a way to say that without being too insulting, Brandon's phone began to ring again.

"Should we answer it?" she asked in a whisper. Glancing at Bufo, she noticed that his eyes were larger and rounder than usual. But before the toad could give his opinion, Brandon reached out and lifted the phone off the hook.

"Murdley Residence," he said, his voice muzzy with sleep.

He held the receiver for a moment, then lifted it away from his ear. "Jennifer," he said, "It's for you."

Jennifer felt her heart begin to speed up. "Who is it?"

Brandon put the phone back to his ear and repeated her question. "His name is Elives," he said after a moment.

Jennifer felt a surge of relief. At least it wasn't the woman from the beauty parlor. "Bring the phone up here, Bran, would you?" she croaked.

Brandon stood and lifted the red plastic phone onto the dresser. Jennifer noticed with amusement that his eyes were hardly open. "Thanks, sweetie," she said. "You can lie back down now."

He settled back to the floor without realizing that his sister was now a toad. His thumb finding its way back to his mouth as if guided by radar, he sighed once and was sound asleep again.

Envying his peaceful oblivion, Jennifer squatted beside the receiver. "Hello, Mr. Elives," she said, trying to keep her voice from quaking.

"Jennifer, I just learned that you've been turned into a toad. I need to warn you that the spell is dangerous."

"What do you mean?"

"If you stay in that form for more than ten hours, the change will be permanent."

An icy fear crept into Jennifer's heart. How much time did she have? She had put Brandon to bed at eight. So it couldn't have been later than 8:10 when Skippy kissed her.

Which meant that at a little after six in the morning she would become a toad forever.

"What can I do?" she asked urgently.

Mr. Elives' response sounded impatient. "You

have realized that the kiss can be passed on, haven't you?"

"Yes."

"Well, keep passing it around until a more permanent solution comes along. Find a friend to share it with. *Just make sure that no one stays a toad for more than nine hours and fifty-nine minutes.*"

"We can't go on doing that forever!" said Jennifer desperately.

"It will have to do until something better comes along," snapped the old man. "Listen, opportunities are all around you. Most people simply don't realize they are there. Keep looking, keep listening, keep thinking. The answer will present itself. Let me speak to Bufo."

"Certainly," said Jennifer. Slightly dazed, and a little angry, she turned to Bufo and said, "He wants to talk to you."

Bufo hopped over and squatted next to the phone. "Hey, boss," he said, trying to sound cheerful. Though Jennifer could not make out the words coming from the receiver, the tone and the volume, and the way Bufo winced, gave her a pretty good idea of the kind of thing Mr. Elives might be saying. Bufo kept trying to respond, but never seemed to be able to get past, "Yes, but . . ." and "Well, I didn't . . ."

Jennifer was astonished at the idea of someone being able to outtalk Bufo. But suddenly the expression on the toad's face changed. His eyes went wide, and he listened more intently. Then he blinked, and Jennifer could tell that the line had gone dead.

"What did he say?" she asked.

"He's annoyed with me for kissing Sharra to begin with. I swear I had no idea that it would turn her into a toad. She's the first human I ever kissed, and that was only to annoy her. It's not as if I find her attractive or anything. Anyway, once he finished bawling me out, he said, 'The wheel is turning, hearts are burning, what's worth learning is never free.' I tried to ask what the heck that meant, but he hung up."

"Is he always like that?"

"Yeah, he likes to keep people on their toes. Part of that 'air of mystery' he likes to cultivate."

"Where is he now?"

Bufo shrugged. "He could be anywhere. He moves that shop around like a con man shuffling shells and peas. What I don't know is if he's the one who decides where to go, or if he's taking orders from someone else. I do know you can't find the place if he doesn't want you to. So he must have had some reason for letting *you* come in."

"I suppose he let me in so that I could get turned into a toad," said Jennifer bitterly. "I just wish I could figure out what I did to deserve this."

"Don't be silly," said Bufo. "Things aren't over yet."

"Right," said Jennifer. "Which means there's still a chance that they can get worse."

"You may think that's happened already when you hear my next idea," said Bufo.

Jennifer swallowed nervously—an interesting sensation when done with a toad's throat. "What is it?" she asked.

"Give me a kiss."

"I knew it!" she cried. "I knew I was going to have to kiss you before this was all over!"

"You don't have to kiss me if you don't want to!" said Bufo, sounding hurt. "I just thought that it might reverse things. You know—one kiss turns you into a toad, the second one turns you back."

"Do you really think so?" asked Jennifer suspiciously.

"I have no idea," said Bufo. "I told you, I never kissed a human until that little blond bombshell got me so annoyed. It's just a thought."

"Wouldn't Mr. Elives have mentioned it if that was true?" asked Jennifer.

"Not necessarily. He might not know. And if he did, he might not tell. He's big on letting people work things out for themselves."

"How do I know it won't just double-toad me?" asked Jennifer.

"You don't!" said Bufo, his voice tinged with exasperation. "Look, it's not my life's ambition to kiss you. I'm just making an offer."

Jennifer sighed. *I may be the only kid on earth so ugly even a toad doesn't want to kiss me,* she thought bitterly.

"Well?" asked Bufo.

"I'm *thinking!*"

"Don't blow a brain cell on my account," he snapped.

"All right, all right! Let's try it."

Gathering her courage, she hopped closer to Bufo. "Just a little one," she said nervously.

"You're the boss," replied Bufo, pursing his lips.

Jennifer leaned forward, and planted her lips against his.

No thunder rumbled above them. No cloud of smoke formed from the air.

Yet a strange sensation jolted through Jennifer's frame. To her astonishment, Bufo jumped backward—something she had never seen a toad do before.

"Good grief," he said, "I had no idea *that* would happen!"

"What?" cried Jennifer. "What is it?"

But she didn't need Bufo to answer. Once she was calm enough to take stock of the situation, she could see for herself what had happened. It wasn't clear if she was more toadly than ever, but she was certainly more of a toad than ever. Exactly twice the toad she had been, in fact—which is to say that she seemed to have doubled in size.

"Remarkable," said Bufo.

" 'Remarkable'!" cried Jennifer. "Is that all you can say? You come up with this stupid 'Kiss me' idea, turn me into the biggest toad in the state, and the best you can come up with is 'remarkable'?"

"Astonishing," said Bufo. "Incredible, amazing, and slightly stupefying. Does that make you feel better?"

"Don't be such a smart aleck," said Jennifer. "What am I going to do now?"

"I'm sure you can get one of the others to change places with you for a while," said Bufo.

"Probably," said Jennifer. "But when I turn back into a human, will I be my usual size, or will I be nine feet tall?"

Bufo shrugged. "I told you, this is all new to me."

Jennifer hopped to the edge of the dresser and stared into the darkness.

TEN

Bang-o, Change-o!

As the returning sun leached the darkness from the sky, Jennifer gazed through her window, thinking about everything that had happened so far.

Soon she was going to have to wake someone and beg them to take her place as a toad. Her only choices at the moment were Ellen, Sharra, or Brandon.

Though she had been horrified when Sharra had been turned into a toad, she had also found it slightly amusing. That was because she had had no idea what it felt like to lose your body and be twisted into a different shape. An *ugly* shape.

Now she knew.

She looked at the floor. Way down. What would happen if she jumped? Was she now immortal, like Bufo? She decided not to test the idea.

She was getting ready to wake the sleepers when Brandon began to stretch and yawn. After a moment, he stood and stared at the two girls still sleeping in her bed.

"Jennifer?" he asked, sounding puzzled.

"Over here, Brandon," she said softly. "On the dresser."

Brandon crossed to the dresser. He stood for a moment, then blinked, shook his head, and cried, "Hey, how'd you do that?"

Jennifer glanced at her clock. It was 5:52. She had less than twenty minutes before the change was permanent. Feeling guilty, even though she knew she could change him back, she said, "Take me outside and I'll show you."

"Okay," said Brandon. He reached forward with both hands to pick her up. "Man, you're the fattest toad I ever saw," he said, once he had her in his grasp.

"Just take me outside," snapped Jennifer. "And be quiet. We don't want to wake anyone up."

Once they were in the backyard, Jennifer said, "All right, here's what we're going to do. I'm going to let you turn into a toad for a minute, so you can see what it's like. Then I'm going to turn you back. All right?"

"Okay!" said Brandon happily.

Trying to keep her sense of guilt from overwhelming her, praying that she would return to her normal size, Jennifer said, "Then give me a little kiss."

Unlike Skippy, Brandon was still fond of kissing the other members of his family. Furthermore, he seemed to have no qualms about kissing a toad. A bang, a flash of light, and the transformation was made. To Jennifer's enormous relief, she was her regular size, not some nine-foot-tall monster.

Sitting at her feet was the cutest little toad she had ever seen. "Bang-o! Change-o!" it cried. "This is neat." Then it began to hop around like mad.

"Brandon!" said Jennifer. "Settle down."

She reached down for him, but he hopped away with a series of improbably high bounces, crying, "Wheee! I'm a toad!"

"Brandon!" she snapped. "Come here. I have to turn you back now."

"No! I wanna be a toad for a while."

Jennifer hesitated, tempted to let him stay a toad for the next several hours, so she wouldn't have to return to that shape. *No,* she told herself, *I can't do that. This is my problem, not Brandon's.*

"Maybe I'll let you be a toad again later, Brandon," she whispered. "But for now I need to turn you back. Mommy might get mad if I don't."

"Why?"

Jennifer was losing her patience. It was hard enough to force herself to do the right thing without Brandon begging her not to. "Because there are things out here that *eat* toads," she said ferociously. Then, toning down her voice, she added, "Let me turn you back and we'll get you some breakfast."

"I want to be a toad," said Brandon stubbornly.

"Mommy will get mad if I leave you this way," said Jennifer—a comment that was an understatement, to say the least. "Do you want a bowl of Sugar-Boogers?"

"Sugar-Boogers" was the name Skippy had given Brandon's favorite breakfast cereal. He had invented it in an attempt to annoy the youngest Murdley. But Brandon liked it, so Skippy had only ended up annoying their parents—which from his point of view was almost as satisfactory.

"Yay for Sugar-Boogers!" cried Brandon.

"Right," said Jennifer, who ate nothing but granola for breakfast herself. "Yay! Now come here."

Brandon hopped over to her, and Jennifer bent down to kiss him. In a flash she was a toad again. She had one small bit of relief; she had feared that when she kissed Brandon, she would end up as big as she had been the last time. But she was only the size she had been with her first transformation. That was good. Being a toad was trouble enough; she had no desire to be an abnormally large one on top of that.

After Jennifer had talked Brandon through the process of getting his bowl of cereal (which they managed to do with only minimal milk slopping), he put her on the table next to him. Soon a fly came buzzing past Jennifer's forehead. Without thinking, she shot out her tongue, pulled the insect in, and swallowed it.

"Hey!" yelled Brandon. "How come you get to eat bugs? Everyone yells when I do it."

"It was an accident," said Jennifer, feeling

queasy. "Besides, I'm a toad. Toads are *supposed* to eat bugs."

"See!" said Brandon. "I knew it was fun being a toad! I wanna be a toad again!"

Jennifer was too busy trying not to throw up to argue with him. After Sharra's extravagant display of disgust, she didn't want to put on a big show. But her stomach was doing flip-flops at the idea of what she had just tossed into it.

Before she could get herself under control enough to speak, Mrs. Murdley walked into the kitchen.

Jennifer felt a chill of terror. What was she doing here? Normally she wouldn't be up for hours yet!

And how was she going to react to the discovery that her daughter was a toad?

But of course, Mrs. Murdley didn't look at Jennifer and cry, "Why, dear, what happened? How did you get turned into a toad?" She took one look at her daughter and said, "Brandon, get that toad off the table! You know you're not supposed to have animals up there. How did you get that cereal and milk for yourself, anyway? Why didn't you come and get me if you were hungry?"

"Jennifer help-ted me," said Brandon, smiling broadly.

"Where is Jennifer?" said Mrs. Murdley, tightening the belt on her robe and running a long-fingered hand through her tangled red hair. "I want to talk to her for a minute."

"She's right here," said Brandon, pointing to Jennifer. "This is Jennifer. She's a toad."

"Oh, Bran," said Mrs. Murdley, kneeling beside her youngest son. "You know how sensitive Jennifer is about her looks. I know she isn't beautiful, honey, but you shouldn't name this toad after her. It will really hurt her feelings."

Not any more than you have already, thought Jennifer, trying to stifle the sob she felt building inside her. It came out in a strangled form that made Mrs. Murdley jump. "What was that?" she asked.

"I don't know," said Brandon. "Jennifer did it."

"Brandon," said Mrs. Murdley, "I *don't* want you to call this toad by your sister's name. Now either take it outside, or go put it in that terrarium she just made. And tell Jennifer I want to see her."

"Can I finish my Sugar-Boogers first?"

"Don't call them that! And yes, you can finish them. I probably shouldn't talk to Jennifer until I've had some coffee, anyway."

Mrs. Murdley wandered over to the counter and began fumbling with the coffeemaker. As she did, Jennifer held up a short brown finger and pressed it to her lips, telling Brandon to be quiet.

He nodded, finished his cereal, scooped up Jennifer, and left the room.

"Brandon!" yelled Mrs. Murdley, as he left the room. "Tell Jennifer I want to see her *now!*"

"Okeydokey," he said, stifling a giggle.

Mrs. Murdley leaned her head against the cupboard and groaned.

107

"Brandon," whispered Jennifer, as soon as they were out of her mother's earshot, "take me outside."

"Okeydokey," he said happily.

"Do you really want to be a toad again?" Jennifer asked, once they were standing under the big oak in the backyard.

"Bang-o! Change-o!" cried Brandon, throwing his arms into the air with a happy smile.

So Jennifer kissed him.

"Now listen," she whispered, as she carried him back toward the house, "don't talk in front of Mommy. It will upset her if you do."

She chose her words carefully. If she had said their mother would scream, or faint, Brandon might have been tempted to say a few words, just to watch the reaction. But he didn't like it when their mother was upset, so she thought that would keep him quiet.

With Brandon in her blouse pocket, Jennifer slipped into the kitchen, where she found her mother staring at the coffeemaker as if it had just been delivered from another planet.

"Brandon said you wanted to see me."

Mrs. Murdley gazed at Jennifer for a moment before answering. "Can you keep an eye on him for me today?" she said at last. "I picked up a cold last night, and I feel as if there's a herd of buffalo wandering around inside my head."

Jennifer hesitated. It would be hard to keep an eye on Brandon if she was a toad. But the other option, that she leave Brandon as a toad, would probably not please her mother, either.

"Jennifer, did you hear me?"

"I heard you, Mom. I'll be glad to take care of him."

"Good. Now where's Brandon gone? I want to tell him what's going on."

"Just a minute, I'll get him," said Jennifer. Leaving the room, she ran outside, pulled Brandon out of her pocket, and gave him a kiss. "Now go back in and see Mom," she said, as soon as he was himself and she was a toad.

"No! I wanna be a toadie again!"

"Go see Mom, and then I'll turn you back!" said Jennifer firmly.

Brandon began trotting toward the house.

"But don't leave me here!" screamed Jennifer.

Brandon ran back to pick her up.

"Ribit!" said Brandon, half an hour later, as he hopped around on top of Jennifer's desk. "Ribit!"

"Toads don't say 'ribit,' " said Bufo.

"I do!" Brandon replied gleefully.

"You can't leave him a toad, Jennifer," said Ellen, though it was clear she was amused by the way Brandon's antics were beginning to annoy Bufo.

"I know I can't leave him a toad," said Jennifer sharply, injured that her best friend would suggest she might even consider such a rotten idea. "I told you no one can stay a toad for more than ten hours. But right now he's enjoying it!"

" 'sfun!" said Brandon. "I wanna eat a bug!"

"That kid is gross," said Sharra, who was trying to comb her hair. She shook her head irritably. "Don't you have a mirror in here?"

"No, I don't, and no, he's not!" snapped Jennifer, though she wished Brandon would stop talking about eating bugs. She remembered all too clearly the taste of the one she had eaten herself less than an hour ago.

"I'm not gross," said Brandon, "I'm a toad! Ribit!"

Jennifer picked him up and put him in the shoe box. "Come on," she said, "we have to go someplace."

"Where?"

"The Folk Museum. I have an appointment with Miss Applegate this morning, and I'm hoping she may know some things about toads and spells and so on. Anyone else want to come?"

"I'd like to," said Ellen, "but my mother told me I have to be home by ten. We're going to visit my grandmother."

"I'll come," said Sharra.

Jennifer looked at her in surprise.

"I don't have anything else to do," she said with a shrug. "This might be amusing."

"I think I'll stay here," said Bufo. "I didn't get much sleep last night. And one of us ought to be here in case Elives calls."

"Are you sure you want to answer the phone?" asked Jennifer. "It might be the other one, that woman from the beauty parlor."

"What's she going to do?" asked Bufo. "Powder me to death? Make my lips stick?"

"Now there's an idea," said Jennifer.

"Just put the phone beside my tank and be on your way," said Bufo.

Jennifer left a note on the counter to remind her parents that she had already discussed the trip to the Folk Museum with them and to let them know that Brandon was going with her.

In the garage, still slightly astonished that Sharra was coming along, she found herself offering to let her enemy use her new bike. "I can take this one," she said, referring to the slightly-too-small bike that the new one had replaced.

As she pedaled along, her knees sticking out to the side, Jennifer tried to figure out what it was that had prompted her to let Sharra ride the new bike. Was it all the lectures her mother had given her about being nice? Or was it her own sense of worthlessness, which seemed to rise to the surface whenever she was in the presence of someone as beautiful as Sharra?

She was still trying to puzzle that out when they reached the museum.

"Good morning, Jennifer," called Miss Applegate when they walked through the door. "I'm so glad you remembered our appointment. I've been gathering information for you."

"Thanks," said Jennifer, turning her head away from the mirror in the foyer. Walking to Miss Applegate's desk, she accepted the thick manila folder the old woman held out to her, then said, "I hope you don't mind, but I have a new question for you."

"That's what I'm here for. What do you want to know?"

"Do you have any folklore about toads?"

"Toads?" asked Miss Applegate. She sounded puzzled, almost as though she had never heard the word before.

"You know," said Sharra. "Warty little animals that croak."

Miss Applegate widened her eyes. "I *know* what toads are," she said sharply. "If you'll be patient, I'll see what I can find."

"Boy, what pushed her buttons?" whispered Sharra as Miss Applegate walked away.

"She's probably not used to people being so rude," replied Jennifer.

Sharra looked surprised. "Do you think I'm rude?"

Jennifer felt as surprised as Sharra looked. "Do you think you're not? I thought you did it on purpose."

Sharra's eyes flashed, but before she could say anything, Brandon shouted, "I want to get out now!"

Jennifer lifted the lid of the shoe box. "You'll have to wait a few minutes, Bran," she whispered. "And try to be quiet. We want to keep you a secret. Okay?"

"I don't wanna be a secret. I wanna get out and play!"

"Why don't I take him outside and let him play on the grass while you do your work," said Sharra.

"Are you sure?"

"Sure I'm sure. He's a cute kid. He's even a cute toad. I don't mind keeping an eye on him for a bit."

Jennifer hesitated. "Well, okay. But be careful of him."

"Look, I'm not a total jerk, Murdley."

"I wanna go outside!" yelled Brandon.

"Okay, okay," said Jennifer. "I'll see you in a few minutes."

Taking the shoe box with Brandon in it, Sharra headed for the door. Moments later Miss Applegate returned, carrying a stack of books and clippings about toads. Jennifer began to read them eagerly. But her enthusiasm soon began to waver.

"There's not much about magic in here," she said sadly, as she sifted through paragraph after paragraph about how toads could be used to predict rain or cure horses.

"What exactly were you looking for?" asked Miss Applegate.

Jennifer hesitated. "I'm not sure. Something a little more—I don't know—a little more *interesting*."

Miss Applegate smiled sadly. "Still looking for a magical answer?"

"What do you mean?"

"For being beautiful. I've seen you stare at the pictures in books, dear. And I've seen the way you avoid the mirror in the hallway. I think I know

how you feel. It would be nice to be pretty like Sharra. But it's not the only thing in life."

Jennifer stared at the old woman. The ugly old woman. She knew what she was saying. They were alike: a pair of uglies.

The thought of being put in the same category as Miss Applegate—"Poor Miss Applegate," as her mother often called her—was more than she could bear. "Don't talk like that!" she said. To her horror, she felt tears streaming down her face. Grabbing the folder, she ran from the museum.

Things were no better outside. As she stumbled down the steps, not certain where she was intending to go, Sharra started after her.

"Jennifer!" she cried, "Jennifer! I'm sorry!"

Jennifer stopped when she realized that Sharra was crying, too. "What's wrong with *you?*" she asked, wiping her sleeve across her eyes.

"I don't know how it happened," babbled Sharra. "I kept my eye on him all the time he was out of the box. Honest!"

"What are you saying?" cried Jennifer in horror.

"It's Brandon," whispered Sharra. "He's gone."

ELEVEN

Desperately Seeking Brandon

Jennifer felt a fear unlike anything she had ever experienced before. Her stomach seemed to have plunged to a place she didn't know it could reach. She could scarcely take the next breath.

Forcing herself to remain calm she asked, "What do you mean—gone?"

"I don't know how it happened," repeated Sharra. "I kept an eye on him all the time he was out of the box, I swear I did. So it's not like someone stepped on him—"

"Don't say that!" snapped Jennifer, who had already had several terrible thoughts about what might have happened to the tiny toad she had made of her baby brother.

Sharra gulped and wiped at her eyes. "He got tired, and I put him back in the box. And I put the lid on. *I know I did.* Then I sat on the steps for a while. A woman came by and talked to me for a minute. After she was gone, I sat here for a few more minutes. Then I got bored, so I decided to talk to Brandon. But when I opened the box, he was gone."

Panic held Jennifer in a grip so real it was as if someone had grabbed her heart with a hand of ice.

"He's hiding," she said, pushing away the fear. "That's got to be it. He loves to hide from me."

"Do you really think so?" sniffled Sharra.

"It has to be," said Jennifer fiercely. "Brandon!" she cried. "Brandon, where are you?"

No answer.

Flinging herself over the side of the steps, she began to crawl along the edge of the building.

"Brandon, this isn't funny," she said, pushing aside stones and moving clumps of grass. "Come on, Bran. Stop hiding. We have to go home now, sweetie. Come on out."

To Jennifer's astonishment, Sharra joined her. "Come on, Brandon," she called. "Tell us where you are. What does he like?" she said, turning to Jennifer.

"Sugar-Boogers! Tell him we'll give him Sugar-Boogers."

"What?"

"It's what we call his favorite cereal."

Sharra looked at her. "You sure have a weird family, Murdley."

"We can discuss my family later. Right now, we have to find Brandon."

Sharra nodded. "Sugar-Boogers," she started to croon. "Come on, Brandon. Tell us where you are and we'll give you some Sugar-Boogers."

Still no answer.

Jennifer's fear, which had briefly ebbed with the thought that Brandon was merely playing a game, began to return stronger than ever. *Had something eaten him?*

"*Brandon!*" she screamed. "*Where are you?*"

"Jennifer, what's the matter?"

It was Miss Applegate. She was standing at the door of the museum, her homely face twisted with concern.

"It's my little brother," said Jennifer. "He was out here with Sharra. She was supposed to be watching him, and now he's gone!"

"Oh, my," said Miss Applegate. "Are you sure he didn't decide to wander on home? Children do that sometimes, you know."

He's not a kid, he's a toad! Jennifer wanted to say. But she knew if she said that, Miss Applegate would think she was playing some kind of stupid game. And maybe the old woman was right. It was possible Brandon had gotten bored and decided to head for home. If so, they had to find him fast, before he was discovered by a predator, or caught by some kid, or run over, or—or—the possibilities were endless, and awful.

"I'm sure no one took him," continued Miss Applegate. "Smokey Hollow just isn't that kind of town."

At those words Jennifer's heart sank. No one *took* him? How about the woman Sharra had been talking to? Could she have taken Brandon?

But why?

Unless—unless she was the woman they had met at the beauty parlor yesterday.

"Sharra!" she said. "That woman you were talking to. What did she look like?"

"Oh, she was pretty," said Sharra. "Really beautiful, actually. She had wonderful long black hair and—"

"That's it!" cried Jennifer. "Don't you remember her from yesterday?"

"What do you mean?"

"The woman in the beauty parlor!"

"I never saw her," said Sharra slowly. "I was in your . . ." She glanced at Miss Applegate. "I didn't have a chance to see her. Remember?"

Jennifer groaned. Of course—Sharra had been tucked in the pouch of her sweatshirt all during that conversation.

"Jennifer?" said Miss Applegate uncertainly.

"It's all right," said Jennifer, trying to sound reassuring. "I think I know what happened to him. Come on, Sharra—let's go."

Sharra looked at her as if she had lost her mind.

"Come *on*, Sharra," she repeated fiercely. "Let's go."

Sharra nodded, and the two girls hopped on their bikes and shot away from the Folk Museum.

"Where are we going?" gasped Sharra when they were a couple of blocks from the museum. "What's going on, anyway? Do you know where Brandon is?"

"First stop is my house," said Jennifer. "I think

I know who has Brandon. But I'm not sure how to get there. If that so-called beauty parlor is anything like Mr. Elives' magic shop, it could be anywhere. I'm hoping Bufo will be able to help us."

Secretly, she was hoping they might be able to use the little red phone to get hold of Mr. Elives and ask *him* for help. But that idea seemed like such a long shot she was afraid of jinxing the possibility by saying it out loud.

"Why does that woman want Brandon, anyway?" asked Sharra.

"I don't know," said Jennifer, who had been wondering the same thing herself. If it was only to get a toad that had some magical properties, then perhaps Brandon would fit the bill. If that were so, the woman would have no reason to make the beauty parlor visible again. Jennifer shivered. If that was the case, they would never find the beauty parlor.

Their only hope was that what the woman really wanted was Bufo, probably for the jewel in his forehead, and that she was going to ask for a trade. Yet it was a strange and terrible hope, for though Jennifer knew she would trade Bufo for her brother in a moment, she also felt there was something deeply wrong about just handing the toad over to someone else.

And if she did hand him over to the Mistress of the Beauty Parlor of Doom, heaven alone knew what Mr. Elives would do once he found out about it.

To Jennifer's surprise, Skippy and Ellen were waiting in front of the house when they arrived. Bufo was with them, sitting on Ellen's shoulder.

"What are you doing here?" Sharra said to Ellen. "I thought you had to go someplace."

"Skippy called my house, looking for you two. When he told me what was going on . . ."

"What *is* going on?" asked Jennifer in confusion.

"*You* lost Brandon, that's what's going on," said Skippy, his voice heavy with accusation.

"How do you know about that?" cried Jennifer, struck by a new surge of panic. She had hoped to get Brandon back before anyone else knew he was gone. "Anyway," she added, "it wasn't me who lost him, it was Sharra."

"I didn't lose him!" cried Sharra. "He ran away!"

"Shut up, all of you," roared Bufo, in a voice that must have been modeled on a sergeant major's. "We have work to do."

They shut.

"All right," Bufo said, when everyone had settled down, "first we need to fill each other in. I'll start. About twenty minutes ago Brandon's phone rang. I figured it was Elives, but I was wrong; it was that woman you met yesterday. She has your little brother, but she's willing to make a trade."

"For what?" asked Jennifer nervously.

Bufo hesitated. "For me," he said at last.

Jennifer nodded grimly. "I suspected that. What are we going to do?"

"Make the trade," said Bufo, his voice equally grim.

"But what will she do with *you?*" asked Ellen.

Bufo shrugged. "I don't know. A number of possibilities come to mind, none of them pleasant. That's a secondary problem. Right now we have to get Brandon back."

"You're not kidding we have to get him back," said Skippy. "Ellen told me about the time thing. If he doesn't kiss someone before tonight, he's a toad forever."

"Maybe we should call the police," said Ellen nervously.

"I wish we could," said Bufo. "But this woman, this witch, whoever she is, said that if we ever want to see Brandon again, we come alone. Kids only. Kids and one toad. Otherwise she picks up her beauty parlor and goes home."

"How are we supposed to find the place?" asked Sharra.

"She said we were to walk along Beech Street. When we get close enough, she'll let us in."

"Let us in?" asked Ellen.

Bufo shrugged. "I'm just telling you what she said."

They rode their bikes to Beech Street, then got off and walked.

"It's somewhere around here that things keep

going wonky," said Jennifer, as they passed a house that looked familiar.

"I don't like this," said Sharra. "I don't recognize any of it."

"That's because the last time we came here you were a toad and you were hiding in Jennifer's sweatshirt pouch," said Ellen.

"You three sure have been getting into some weird stuff," said Skippy.

Jennifer couldn't tell if what she heard in his voice was fear or envy, or some strange combination of both.

And then, so quickly that no one could identify the moment that it happened, they were no longer on Beech Street, but on some other street that looked perfectly normal but was not part of Smokey Hollow at all.

"Who do you suppose lives in these houses?" whispered Jennifer.

"I don't want to know," replied Ellen.

"They may be only illusion," croaked Bufo, his voice much quieter than usual.

Jennifer understood why he was quiet. Ahead of them she could see the beauty parlor—the Beauty Parlor of *Death*, as she now thought of it. Inside was her little brother—and a strange woman who had powers that none of them understood. They were about to enter that place. Barring some miracle, when they left, they would be leaving Bufo there, alone with the woman.

Jennifer had been so busy worrying about

Brandon that until this moment what they were about to do hadn't really sunk in. She started to ask Bufo if he was sure he wanted to go through with this. But she couldn't, because there was no point in asking if she didn't mean it. And she didn't. She knew she would do whatever was necessary to get Brandon back, even if it meant sacrificing Bufo.

Or herself.

The bell tinkled as the door swung open.

"Welcome to my parlor," said the woman. She was lounging in a beautician's chair in the center of the room, dressed in a simple black robe that looked as if it had been woven from night and spider webs. "Have you brought me my toad?"

"We've got him," said Jennifer, once she was able to get the dryness out of her throat. "Do you have my brother?"

The woman waved her hand toward a nearby counter, where a piece of black cloth covered a round shape nestled among the combs and shampoo bottles. She snapped her fingers and the cloth vanished. Underneath, in a glass sphere, was a little toad. Jennifer was not sure it was Brandon until he cried, "Jennifer! Skippy! *Get me out of here!*"

His voice, on the edge of tears, went through her heart like a dagger.

"Let him go!" said Jennifer.

"Give me the toad," replied the woman, her voice cool, calm.

"Put me down, Jennifer," said Bufo.

Reluctantly, Jennifer took Bufo out of her sweatshirt pouch and placed him on the floor. He began to hop toward the woman. But he stopped several feet away from her.

"Give them the kid," he said, sounding like John Wayne.

Jennifer started to cross toward Brandon.

"Stay there," hissed the woman. She gestured toward the glass ball. With a flick of her finger she caused it to rise into the air. It began to float toward Jennifer.

"Trade is made," she said, bending down. "Now come here, my fine, fat toad."

"Jennifer," said Skippy. "Crack that thing open and kiss Brandon!"

Snatching the transparent sphere out of the air, Jennifer knelt and smacked it against the floor.

Nothing happened.

"You cheated!" she cried.

"Insurance," responded the woman with a merry laugh. "Once Bufo is in my hands, I'll let you open the sphere."

"Witch," said Bufo fiercely.

"Precisely. And it took a lot of hard work to get here."

"Bufo," said Jennifer desperately, "I've got to get Brandon out of this thing."

Bufo sighed and hopped across the floor. "Got you!" cried the woman, reaching down and snatching him up. "At last, at last, I've got you!"

"Let the boy go," croaked Bufo.

The woman snapped her fingers. The sphere dissolved and Brandon hopped out into Jennifer's hands. Bending over, she gave him a kiss.

Thunder shook the air, and in an instant, Brandon was back and Jennifer was once more a toad.

"You may go now," said the woman.

"Can't you help us?" said Sharra. "We can't keep passing that kiss of toadliness around forever."

"Help you?" asked the woman with a laugh. "Certainly, I'll be glad to help you."

Setting Bufo on the counter she raised her hands and made a gesture in the air, whispering beneath her breath as she did. "There," she said to Jennifer. "That takes care of things. No need to pass the kiss around anymore. The next person you kiss will be a toad forever."

Jennifer stared at the woman in astonishment. If the next person she kissed was going to become a toad forever, then she wouldn't be able to kiss anyone.

Ever.

Which meant that she would be a toad for the rest of her life.

TWELVE

Jewel Thief

"Ignore her," said Skippy. "She's faking."

"Would you like to kiss your sister and find out?" asked the woman sweetly.

Skippy blinked but said nothing.

"Why did you do that?" yelled Ellen. She sounded like she was about to cry.

The woman shrugged. "A slight curse is always useful. You never know what someone will be willing to do to have it removed. Now, I think it's time for all of you to leave."

"Leave?" croaked Jennifer.

"Certainly. I have what I wanted. You have your little brother back. There's no need for you to stay longer."

"But I'm still a toad!"

"And likely to remain one," replied the woman. "But that is not my problem."

"Well, it should be," said a voice from behind them.

Jennifer hopped around as fast as her squat body

would let her. "Miss Applegate! What are you doing here?"

The old woman frowned. "I was worried about Brandon when you and Sharra left the museum this morning," she said. "I felt that you might be in trouble. I had no idea how much trouble!" She turned back to the black-haired woman. "What kind of a person are you, anyway, to do something like this to a child?"

"A very old, very fierce, very desperate person," replied the witch evenly.

Jennifer blinked. *Old?* The witch looked as if she were in her twenties at the most.

"So desperate," continued the woman, her voice rising, "that I would suggest you gather these children and take them with you before I do something that makes you wish you were *all* toads!"

"Not until you turn Jennifer back into herself!" shouted Sharra.

"Frankly, I'm not sure that I can," said the black-haired woman. "And even if I wanted to, it would take more work than I'm willing to put into it. Besides, she doesn't need my help. All she has to do is find someone willing to trade places with her!"

"Right," whispered Jennifer. "Should be easy. I know dozens of people just dying to become toads. And I've got the secret—only a kiss away."

She blinked. *Only a kiss away?* An idea began to form in her head.

"You guys should go," she said. "Take Brandon home where he'll be safe. I'm going to stay."

"What?" cried Ellen and Sharra together.

129

"Jennifer, you can't do that," said Skippy.

"Do you think I can go home as a toad?" asked Jennifer. "It's not something Mom and Dad are ready to cope with. But it's okay. I don't *like* the real world. I want to stay here."

The witch looked at Jennifer with new interest. "That's an interesting thought. There are ways in which you might be useful, my dear."

"Jennifer," said Miss Applegate, "I can't let you . . ."

"You don't understand," said the witch. "Inside these doors, I'm the one who lets or doesn't let; I make the rules. You don't get in unless I let you— or unless I make a mistake, as when I left the gate open for these children, and you slipped through, you old hag."

"Hey," said Jennifer. "Don't talk to her like that!"

"Quiet!" snapped the witch, and Jennifer realized that if she was to have any chance at all, she had better do as the woman said.

"And now," she shrieked, waving her hands, "I want you *out!*"

A strong wind began to blow inside the shop, the gusts so fierce they pushed Ellen, Sharra, Skippy, Brandon, and Miss Applegate right across the floor.

"Jennifer!" she heard as her friends went sliding toward the door. "Jennniiifffeeerrrrr!"

And then they were gone.

———

"Alone at last," said the witch with a smile.

"My heart's desire fulfilled," sneered Bufo.

"Listen, sonny, don't be flip or this may turn out to be more unpleasant for you than it needs to be."

Bufo turned to Jennifer. "Sorry I got you into this, kid," he said, using his best Bogart imitation.

"It's not your fault," said Jennifer, wishing everyone would just go away for a few minutes so that she could think. But she didn't have a few minutes. Hopping forward, she looked up at the witch and asked, "What are you going to do to him?"

"Just a little minor surgery. I want the jewel he carries in his forehead."

"Hey!" said Bufo. "I've had that for a long time! I don't think I want to part with it."

"What you want is not an issue," replied the witch.

"What jewel?" asked Jennifer, trying to sound innocent.

Bufo looked at her in surprise, started to say something, then closed his mouth.

"The toad has a jewel in his forehead," said the witch. "One of only two such jewels in all the world, and the only one available now. It is said to provide perfect happiness to the person who possesses it. I intend to possess it."

"What will happen to Bufo when you take it out?" asked Jennifer nervously.

The witch smiled. "Wait and see," she said slyly.

"Based on what happened the last time, I think you'll find the results quite—interesting."

What does she mean by that? wondered Jennifer nervously. Out loud she said, "Do you mean I can watch?"

"No reason not to. Depending on what I decide to do with you, it could be good training." Bending, she scooped Jennifer into her hands, then deposited her on the countertop, a few feet from Bufo.

"How come Bufo has the only jewel?" asked Jennifer, genuinely puzzled this time. "Is he that special?"

Despite himself, Bufo puffed a bit with pride.

"Oh, he certainly is," replied the woman. "There were only two such toads in all the world."

"Where did they come from?"

"My mouth," said the woman, turning and smiling a broad, terrifying smile.

"Mom?" Bufo cried in astonishment. "Is it really you?"

Jennifer blinked. "But that would make you more than five hundred years old!" she said.

"That's right," said the woman.

"But you're so beautiful . . ."

"You can learn a lot in five hundred years," said the woman. "The outside is fairly easy to change. It's the inside that takes work. Would you like to see my real face?"

Terrified yet fascinated, Jennifer whispered, "Yes."

The woman turned away for a moment. When she turned back, Jennifer could not help but cry out in dismay. She had never seen anyone so ugly in her life. The woman's long nose had a big hairy wart on the end of it. Her pointed chin had another. Her lank gray hair hung over the black shawl that she had draped over her hunched shoulders. When she smiled, you could see five yellowed teeth—five, and no more—poking out from grayish pink gums. Beneath her bushy gray brows glittered a pair of black eyes that seemed to look right into your soul.

Her reflection was repeated over and over in the mirrors that lined the room.

"You can get awfully old in five hundred years," said the old woman. "But there are ways to cover it up."

She turned, turned back, and the hag was gone. In her place was the beautiful young woman again.

"What about the curse?" asked Bufo. "I thought you couldn't speak without something crawling out of your mouth."

"Ah, now you get to the root of things," said the woman sweetly. Jennifer stared, trying to find the hag's face beneath the beauty. But it was as if the transformation had never occurred.

"What do you mean?" asked Bufo.

"I mean that you get to the root of why I became a witch at all," she said opening a drawer and pulling out a handful of tweezers. "Once I recovered from the initial shock of the curse, I learned to hold my tongue, so to speak, for the most part. I only opened my mouth to eat or when I was surprised into speaking. But curses can be counterproductive. I suppose that crone in the woods who first cursed my tongue with the vermin spell intended to teach me a lesson. Well, I learned many lessons in the long run. But they all came from the witch who finally took me on as an apprentice."

Spreading the tweezers on the counter before her, she began to point at them with one neatly manicured fingertip.

"I need to choose my tools carefully," she said, half to Jennifer, half to herself. "As a comrade of mine once said, 'These things must be done delicately.' Ah—this should do just fine."

Lifting the largest pair, she held them to the light.

"I still don't understand," said Bufo.

It was clear to Jennifer that he was stalling for time. *Probably clear to the witch, too,* she thought. *But I guess when you're five hundred years old, a few minutes one way or the other doesn't make that much difference.*

"In order to get the spell removed, I had to find someone who had the knowledge to remove it," said the woman. "Which in this case meant I had to find a witch. She took me on as an apprentice. But the fee was high: I had to bring her a Jewel of Perfect Happiness. When I asked her where to find it—spitting out a few spiders and snakes in the process—she told me that the first two toads to come forth from my mouth, one male, one female, each carried such a jewel in their foreheads. All I had to do was find one of the toads,

remove the jewel, and she would teach me everything she knew—including how to control the curse."

"Esmerelda!" cried Bufo, and this time there was no trace of an imitation, only his own voice, thick with grief and loss. "You stole my Esmerelda. *What did you do to her?*"

"The same thing I'm about to do to you," replied the witch calmly.

"Where is she?" demanded Bufo, his grief giving way to anger. "Is she alive?"

"I don't have the slightest idea," said the witch, her voice calm, unruffled.

"But how can you do this to him?" said Jennifer. "I mean, he's like your kid or something!"

The witch turned to Jennifer. "There's always more where he came from," she said softly, her eyes glittering, cold, deadly.

"What do you mean?" whispered Jennifer.

"I told you, the spell is under control. Not gone. Just under"—here she paused for a moment, closed her eyes, and then finished the sentence—"control."

As she spoke the last word, a rat tumbled out of her mouth, dropping to the floor at her feet.

"Run for your life!" cried Bufo.

Eyes wide with astonishment, the rat scurried across the floor and disappeared behind the cabinet.

Jennifer shivered. The witch opened her eyes.

"Disgusting, isn't it?" she asked, her voice bitter. "I have to constantly be on the alert to keep it from happening. Means I tend to keep to myself a lot. One slip in polite company, one careless word at a tea party, one toad in a teacup, and I'm not invited back. It's been a lonely few centuries. I think I'm about due a little happiness. I've always regretted giving away that first jewel. After all, it came out of *my* mouth, even if it was wrapped in a toad when it arrived. So it should have been mine. Fortunately, I knew there was one more available— one more chance at perfect happiness.

"And now I've found it," she said, stepping toward Bufo, the tweezers outstretched before her.

The Temptation
of Jennifer Murdley

"Bufo!" cried Jennifer, hopping across the counter. "Kiss me!"

Bufo looked at her in astonishment.

"What do you think you're doing?" shrieked the witch.

"Kiss me, you fool!" said Jennifer.

Suddenly Bufo understood. Lunging forward, he planted a kiss on Jennifer's lips.

"Again!" she cried. "Again! Again! Again!"

"Stop!" screamed the witch. "Stop!"

But it was too late. The transformation was nearly instantaneous. With every kiss Jennifer doubled in size—from four inches to eight, from eight to sixteen, from sixteen to thirty-two.

With the fourth kiss she was more than five feet long.

The fifth kiss turned her into a toad the size of a Volkswagen.

"Stop!" screamed the witch again, and she raised

her hands to cast a spell. But before she could speak a word, make a gesture, Jennifer's tongue shot forward, pinned the witch's arms to her sides, and drew her back into Jennifer's mouth, where she was held fast, her feet sticking out of one side, her head out of the other.

"Well, that was very good," said Bufo. "My congratulations."

Jennifer looked at him but said nothing, as it was difficult to speak with a mouthful of witch.

The witch noticed the problem immediately. "What are you going to do, Jennifer?" she asked, her voice soft, wheedling. "You can't keep me this way forever. Are you going to spit me out—or swallow me? I don't know about swallowing; I might get stuck in your throat. I could do a lot of damage before I'm done, or down, or whatever."

"Ignore her, Jennifer," said Bufo desperately. "She's got a voice like honey; she could talk a cat into a doghouse."

"That's not entirely wrong," said the witch. "And I can do more than that. I can offer a trade. Look around you, Jennifer. Look in the mirrors, and let me show you what might be. Remember, I have powers, I can change things. Look at yourself."

From every mirror in the shop stared a giant toad, a witch dangling from its mouth.

ME! thought Jennifer, in fear and revulsion.

But even as she stared at the mirrors, the image began to shift. First the toad dissolved. In its place stood a familiar image, one Jennifer had tried to see as little as possible over the last few years: her own plain face with its small eyes, big nose, and puffy cheeks, framed as always by limp, mousy hair. How she hated that image!

But as she watched, it began to shift: The nose shrank, the eyes grew. The limp hair became a thick, shaggy mane of sun yellow as the cheeks narrowed and slimmed. Cheekbones rose beneath those cheeks, like mountains stirring beneath the earth's crust, and beauty crept across her face like dawn across the sea.

Great tears formed in Jennifer-the-toad's enormous eyes. This was the secret image she had held within, the way she would have chosen to look, if only she had the power.

"*I* have the power," whispered the witch, as if she had read Jennifer's mind. "I can make you look like that if you want; if you're willing to trade. Just say the word, Jennifer. Let me go. I can make you human again. And not merely your old, ugly self. I can make you beautiful . . ."

Jennifer hopped forward, a leap that covered several feet. The image in the mirror, not that of a toad, but of a girl more beautiful than Sharra, came forward to greet her.

The Jennifer that might be, the midnight dream that haunted her days.

"*Beautiful* . . . ," whispered the witch.

"Jennifer," said Bufo desperately. "Don't listen to her! Remember what she—"

"Quiet, you," hissed the witch.

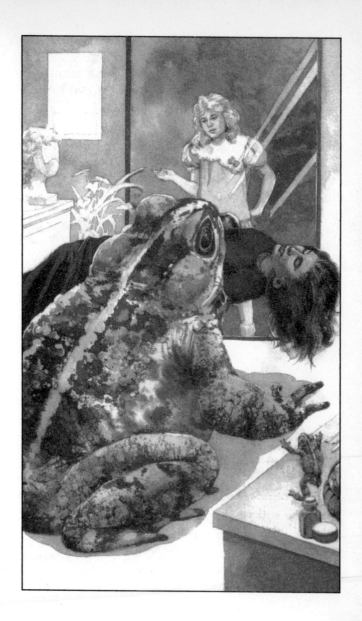

Ignoring her anger, Bufo tried again. "Remember what she really—"

"Quiet!" bellowed the witch. Losing control in her wrath, she spit out not only the word but another rat, which came hurtling out of her mouth and landed halfway across the room.

Jennifer-the-toad took another step toward the mirror. Jennifer-the-beautiful stepped forward to meet her.

"This is what you look like inside," whispered her reflected self, and Jennifer could not tell whether the words were spoken aloud or only in her mind. "Like the geode. Let me out. She can help you—help *us*. She can set me free, release the beauty inside you."

Like the geode, thought Jennifer, her mind whirling as if lost in some fever dream. *But if you turn it inside out, it's beautiful outside, and ugly inside.*

"Where does beauty matter?" whispered the reflection. "Where you can see it! What else counts?"

"Barbie and Ken!" bellowed Bufo. "Perfect plastic people! Is that what you want, Jennifer? If that's it, go ahead. Spit the witch out. She can have the jewel in my head, and let what happens happen."

I don't want to trade you for being beautiful, thought Jennifer, still unable to open her mouth, for fear of letting the witch escape. *But oh, how I want to look like that. Oh, how I want to be beautiful.*

If only someone would make the decision for her.

But no one would.

"It's your choice," whispered the mirror.

"Decide, Jennifer," hissed the witch. "Give me the toad, and I'll let you go free—free and as beautiful as you could wish."

Jennifer sat in silence, her mouth closed.

"He's only a toad," wheedled the witch. "And a rude one at that. It's not as if I want your brother; I only got him by accident, anyway. I thought I was stealing this one. But your brother did make a perfect trading card—I gave you the child, you gave me the toad. You were willing to sacrifice the toad for your brother. Why not for yourself? He's only a toad, Jennifer. Only a toad."

Only a toad, thought Jennifer. But the words burned, because she had heard words like them too many times, sneered once by Sharra, and whispered over and over in her memory thereafter. *A toad for a toad.*

In the mirror, the witch's image appeared beside that of the Jennifer-that-could-be. She was as beautiful as night, with eyes you could drown in.

"Or you could join me," the witch whispered, putting her arm around the false reflection. "Stay with me and learn the secrets I have to offer. *I* traded the jewel of happiness for them. All *you* have to trade is a single toad. I get the jewel, you get the beauty and wisdom and immortality. And Bufo gets to go on living, only slightly—altered. Why not, Jennifer? Why not stay with me and learn my secrets? Look at me. See how beautiful I am? See how beautiful you can be? Stay with me. Be beautiful. Stay with me . . ."

Jennifer ached with the sight of the self that could be, the face in the mirror that had, until now, existed only in her imagination.

Only a toad, she thought. *He's only a toad. I only met him two days ago, and life has been nothing but trouble since. I don't owe him a thing. And he's only a toad, after all. And I could be beautiful . . .*

And then she remembered Mr. Elives' words: "Take good care of this toad. If you don't, you'll have me to answer to."

Would the old man pursue her, punish her, if she traded Bufo in for beauty? What would he do? Would the witch protect her?

"Beautiful," crooned the witch. "So beautiful . . ."

"Most mirrors are mere errors," said Mr. Elives.

Jennifer blinked. Mr. Elives? What was he doing here?

But it wasn't Mr. Elives—it was Bufo, using the old man's voice.

"Shut up!" snarled the witch.

But it was too late. Like sand in butter, the words had grated against something, shaken Jennifer out of her stupor. She stared at herself in the mirror, at the Barbie-perfect image the witch and her imagination had conjured up, and knew it was not, could not, ever *really* be her. With a cry of rage and sorrow, she lashed out at it with her most powerful weapon—her tongue. The great length of solid muscle shot across the room. The witch was still stuck to it. She struck the mirror, which shattered against her back, glass tinkling to the floor.

Unconscious, the witch fell from Jennifer's tongue and lay amid the shards of glass. Yet her image and the image of the false Jennifer remained, surrounding them in all the other mirrors that lined the walls of the shop.

"Jennifer," the images crooned, as if they had taken on a life of their own. "Jennifer, it's not too late. Trade the toad. He's only a toad."

But Jennifer had had enough of mirrors. Nearly blind with rage, she lashed out again and again, her powerful toad's tongue slamming the smooth reflective surfaces, shattering one after another, until suddenly she found herself standing not in a modern beauty parlor but inside a cottage that looked as if it had been lifted from a fairy tale.

"It's my home!" cried Bufo in astonishment. "Jennifer, *this is the cottage where I was born!*"

Jennifer didn't answer; her tongue was sore and bleeding, and speech was more trouble than it was worth.

Bufo seemed to understand. "Let's get out of here," he said, glancing at the unconscious form of the witch.

She nodded, though getting out wasn't going to be easy, since the cottage's only door was less than half her width. She hopped toward it, nudged it with her nose.

Not a chance of getting through.

Turning, she went to the back of the cottage, took a few small, exploratory hops forward, then hurtled her great body at the door.

Struck by two thousand pounds of toad, the door gave way, along with the wall, and Jennifer found herself outside, blinking in the sunlight that flooded the small forest clearing where she had landed.

What happened to the street? she wondered.

Before she could worry about that, a figure stepped from among the trees.

It was Mr. Elives.

"Congratulations," said the old man. "And apologies. When this started, I didn't know what I was getting you into. But you have handled yourself well."

Jennifer considered giving him the same treatment she had given the witch. *A good tongue-lashing may be just what he needs*, she thought. She tried to say it, but her tongue was too sore, and she couldn't get the words out.

"I will take care of the witch," he said.

"*Now* you'll take care of her," said Bufo. "Excuse me, boss, but where were you when we needed you?"

"There are some thresholds I cannot cross," said Mr. Elives, his voice solemn rather than cranky. "And this cottage could not be entered without an invitation, which I surely would never have received. The door is gone, however, knocked down from within, and now I may enter. And I had best do so soon, for there is no knowing how long the woman may sleep. I have work to do if you are to be safe. Follow the path—it will lead you home, where your friends are waiting."

"Home?" cried Jennifer, the word exploding out of her in spite of her injured tongue. "How can I go home like this?"

From inside the cottage came a slight moan.

"Quickly!" said the old man. "Go. Now!"

"But—"

"Now!"

"Jennifer," said Bufo nervously. "We'd better go."

The path led through a forest that seemed older and more gnarled than any Jennifer had ever seen. She moved slowly, the woods too thick for her to take the kind of hops and leaps her great body was capable of.

Thick roots rumpled the soil, and after a while Bufo scrambled onto her back, since it was easier for him to ride than to try to keep up with even her small hops in that terrain.

"I have a question," said Jennifer after a while.

"Shoot," replied Bufo.

"The words you said when we were in the shop—'most mirrors are mere errors.' How did you know them? They were in the letter Mr. Elives sent me."

"You don't really want to know that," said Bufo with a little laugh.

"Yes, I do," replied Jennifer, remembering that Bufo *had* to tell the truth when asked a direct question. "How did you know them?"

Bufo cleared his throat. Using the president's voice, he said, "Well, when you went off to the museum with Brandon this morning, there I was alone in the room with that letter."

"So you read it, even though he didn't want you to," said Jennifer, not really surprised.

"Well, ahhh, I guess you could say . . ."

Before Bufo could finish blathering, Jennifer felt the world go strange around her, and found herself facing a pair of mountain ash trees that looked familiar. On the other side were Sharra and Ellen, Skippy and Brandon, and old Miss Applegate, sitting on the grass beside the bikes, talking quietly among themselves. They looked sad and frightened. Brandon was crying.

Jennifer stopped before she reached the trees. A wave of despair washed over her. "I can't go out there," she said. "I can't go back into our world like this."

"I don't think you should stay here," said Bufo. "Wherever 'here' is."

At the sound of their voices the others looked up. Their reactions to the sight of Jennifer's enormous bulk varied from strangled gasps to near screams. But to her astonishment, rather than running away, they ran *to* her.

"Jennifer?" cried Ellen. "Jennifer, is that you?"

"How did you do that?" asked Brandon, happy

to see his sister in whatever form she chose for her return.

"Mom and Dad are *not* going to like this," contributed Skippy.

Sharra simply stood blinking for a moment. Then, speaking so rapidly that all the words ran into one another, she stepped back and said, "I'm sorry for every rotten thing I ever did to you, Jennifer, so please, *please* don't eat me!"

She was so desperate, and so sincere, that Jennifer nearly laughed in spite of her situation.

Only Miss Applegate didn't speak. She simply walked up to Jennifer, which put them face to face.

Leaning forward, she planted a kiss on Jennifer's yard-wide lips.

The explosion was thunderous.

When the smoke cleared, Jennifer had been returned to her human form and Miss Applegate had been turned into a toad.

Jennifer started to speak, to cry out, "Don't you understand? You're going to be a toad *forever.*"

But before she could say a word Bufo hopped forward. He sat in front of Miss Applegate and stared in astonishment. Then he croaked a single word, which came out as a statement, a question, and a sigh of wonder: *"Esmerelda?"*

Miss Applegate hopped forward to meet him. "It's been nearly five centuries since that witch stole the Jewel of Perfect Happiness from my forehead and turned me into a human, Bufo. Five hundred years of waiting to find you, and all you can say is 'Esmerelda?'"

Bufo smiled. "Give me a kiss," he croaked, sounding only like himself.

And Esmerelda did.

Epilogue

The wind was blowing through the open window.

Jennifer Murdley put the finishing touches on her essay, then placed the geode her father had given her on top of the loose pages to hold them in place.

She could have closed the window, but she was expecting company.

She knew they were coming because she had gotten a call earlier that evening. Not on the regular phone, but on Brandon's little red telephone, which he had generously given to her as a "backward" present on the day of his fourth birthday.

"Jennifer," the voice on the other end of the line had said, "this is Elives. Bufo and Esmerelda want to know if you're going to be in this evening; they'd like to come over to say good-bye."

Jennifer had told Mr. Elives that she would make it a point to be in. He, in return, had told her to set her alarm for midnight.

At 12:15 a high-pitched voice outside her window called, "Rapunzel, Rapunzel, let down your hair, that I might climb the golden stair."

This was followed by another voice that said, "Bufo, cut that out. You don't have to be a clown *all* the time!"

Smiling, Jennifer went to her window and lowered a basket on a rope. After Bufo and Esmerelda climbed in, she hauled the basket back up to her window.

"How have you been, dear?" asked Esmerelda in a voice that sounded like every grandmother in the world combined.

"Pretty well," said Jennifer. "My tongue has healed up, I got my essay finished, Sharra has been leaving me alone, and Skippy seems a little scared of me. So all in all, I guess things are pretty good."

"You could try aiming a bit higher," said Bufo, doing his presidential imitation again.

"Shush!" said Esmerelda.

Despite the fact that Miss Applegate had explained that there had never been an Applegate family, that she had simply used the name, and moved from place to place whenever people got too suspicious because she had been living in one town for too long, Jennifer still had a hard time thinking of the old woman as a toad.

"But I was *always* a toad inside," Miss Applegate had told her the first three times they had had the conversation. "And a lonely one, too, since I thought I was going to live forever without ever seeing Bufo again."

"What a horrible fate!" exclaimed Bufo, zapping out his tongue and swallowing a bug.

And now the two of them were going to leave on their "second honeymoon," though where exactly they were going seemed to be a matter that was known only to Mr. Elives and the two toads.

"We can't talk about it," said Bufo, using his Bogart imitation. "Special assignment."

"Speaking of special assignments," said Esmerelda, "we have one for you, if you're willing to accept it."

"What is it?" asked Jennifer, knowing even as she did so that she was probably letting curiosity overcome common sense.

"Lower the basket again," said Esmerelda.

Looking at the toads nervously, Jennifer did as they asked. When she felt a tug on the slender rope, she pulled the basket back to her window.

Inside were two rats.

Jennifer jumped back with a startled squeak.

"See, Jerome!" said one of them. "I told you she wouldn't like us."

"Don't be ridiculous," said Jerome. "She's just startled."

Suddenly Jennifer remembered the final moments in the cottage. "You came out of the witch's mouth, didn't you?" she asked in astonishment.

"Got it in one, kid," replied Bufo, without giving the rats a chance to answer. "I'd like you to meet the two newest Immortal Vermin, Jerome and Roxanne. Elives wants to know if they can stay with

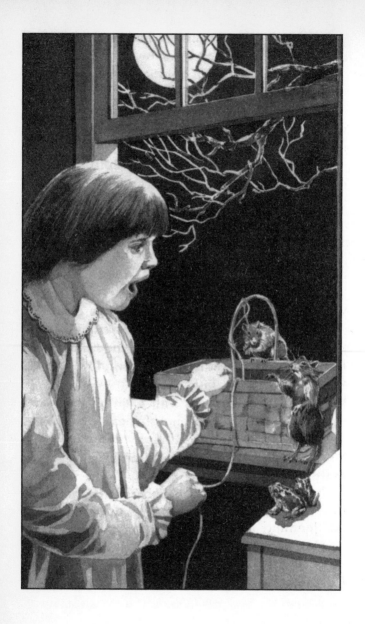

you until he decides what to do with them. After all, the terrarium is empty."

"We don't eat much," said Roxanne sincerely.

"And I know a lot of jokes," said Jerome.

"Quiet," said Roxanne, batting him on the head with her paw. "If she hears any of *your* jokes, she'll never let us stay here."

"Look, if they get to be too much trouble, you can just call Elives and ask him to take them back," said Bufo.

"And how am I supposed to do that?" asked Jennifer.

"Come here," said Esmerelda quietly, motioning to Jennifer to bend closer.

When Jennifer did as she asked, the ancient toad woman whispered a number in her ear.

"Direct connection," she said, when she was sure that Jennifer had it. "I don't think more than five kids in the world can get in touch with the old man whenever they want. But he told me you had earned the privilege."

When the toads were gone and the rats finally settled in to their new home, Jennifer sat and stared at the red phone for a long time.

Suddenly it began to ring. Jennifer hesitated, then lifted the receiver.

"Jennifer?" asked a familiar voice.

"Yes, Mr. Elives, this is Jennifer."

"I just wanted to let you know that Bufo and Esmerelda are safely on their way."

"Will I ever see them again?" she asked, a sudden stab of longing shooting through her.

"I guarantee it. For now, though, you should have your hands full with Jerome and Roxanne. I think you'll like them. They just need a good place to stay while they get used to the world."

"They're welcome here," said Jennifer sincerely.

"I thought they would be," said Mr. Elives. He paused, then said, "You did well, Jennifer. I am pleased with you."

Coming from the old man, the words made Jennifer feel as though she had just been told she was the most wonderful person in the world. Or the most beautiful.

"Thank you," she whispered.

After she hung up, she sat in the dark, her hands resting on the phone. From the other side of the room, she could hear Jerome and Roxanne, squabbling good-naturedly about how they were going to arrange their living quarters.

She remembered Mr. Elives' last words, just before she put down the receiver: "If this works out, I expect that I'll have many assignments for you in the future."

She smiled into the darkness.

It was going to be an interesting life.

Maybe even a beautiful one.

A Note from the Author

One reason I keep writing stories about Mr. Elives' magic shop is that it was the kind of place I had longed to find when I was a kid myself.

The first time I found the shop was when I was writing a book called *The Monster's Ring*. Not long after that book was published, I sat down and made a list of things you could buy in such a place, things that could start an adventure.

My first thought was that I would write a book of short stories called *Tales from the Magic Shop*. Each story would have been about a different character who stumbled into Mr. Elives' shop. But the truth is, I have a hard time with short stories, and the things I write tend to get longer and longer, until eventually they turn into books.

The first time I tried to write the story of Jennifer Murdley, I finished about forty pages, ending with a scene in which the kids looked out Jennifer's window and saw a toad the size of a Volkswagen.

Then I invented an outline for the rest of the story—a complicated plot that involved Mr. Elives being kidnapped, a planet full of toads, and a lizard who made too many puns. I sent the finished chapters and the outline to several editors, who almost unanimously said something along the lines of "*Love* the toad, *hate* the outline."

So, I put the story away for a while (often the smartest thing to do with an idea that is not quite working). What happened next is kind of complicated, but the short version is that my friend Jane Yolen, a famous children's book writer and editor, asked me to do some books for a new line she was starting. I showed her what I had written on Jennifer's story, and her reaction was the same as the other editors who had seen it, with a difference: She figured I could fix the end, and she gave me a contract to write the book.

Now I *had* to come up with a new ending. The only problem was I had no idea what it was going to be.

I went right back to the beginning of the book. From the start, I had known that Jennifer wanted to be special. But it wasn't until this time around—about eight years after I first had the idea for the book—that I realized she wanted to be *beautiful.* Suddenly the book began to make sense to me.

I was interested in writing about the topic of beauty because it is so confusing to me. We all know that beauty is only skin-deep, you should never judge a book by its cover, etc., etc. Now I will make an embarrassing confession: Even though I know those

158

things, I spend a ridiculous amount of time in front of my mirror, studying my looks, trying to figure out if they are good enough. I know this is foolish, but that doesn't stop me. And I am not alone; the culture we live in is obsessed with beauty over brains, skin over soul, heartthrobs over great hearts. I don't have any answers for how we can get past that nonsense, but I thought the issue was at least worth looking at.

The hardest part of writing Jennifer's story was finding an ending. In an old-fashioned fairy tale, she would have gotten her wish and become beautiful at the end. Yecch! An ending like that would have betrayed the whole spirit of the book. It would have betrayed Jennifer. So, in the end she doesn't get her wish. But she does get something else that is, perhaps, just as good.

Maybe even better.

That's the way it goes in this world, at least some of the time.

The Magic Shop Books

Step inside Mr. Elives' magic shop—a place where boys hatch dragons, toads talk, rats deliver messages, and skulls spout Shakespeare. You are sure to find enchantment, adventure, insight, and fun!

"Will bring laughter and near tears . . . Coville offers a fantasy that younger readers can handle easily, and one in which dragons really exist for a little while."

—*School Library Journal*

"A fast-moving, rollicking, yet serious tale . . . Will keep youngsters thinking."

—*School Library Journal*

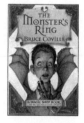

"This lively tale . . . will appeal, at any time, to anyone who, like Russell, is 'very fond of monsters.' "

—*The New York Times Book Review*

"Although humorous, the story has surprising depth, with musings on honor, power, strength, courage, and, above all, love."   —*School Library Journal*

www.brucecoville.com